Restless

By:

Jessica Terry

Restless

Jessica Terry

Published by Jessica Terry, 2020.

RESTLESS

First edition. May 25, 2020.

Copyright © 2020 Jessica Terry.

ISBN: 979-8986432182

Written by Jessica Terry.

PROLOGUE

No one could have prepared Sahara for this news. If someone had told her that morning that her world would be ripped apart at around six o'clock that evening, she would have scoffed at them. But that's exactly what was happening.

She looked into the piercing brown eyes of her husband, Kyle. Eyes that she had loved to gaze into ever since she met him at a basketball game in high school almost eighteen years earlier. They had always showed so much emotion, so much raw desire for her. Now, they were empty. Completely devoid of any feeling or anything at all. Sahara had never seen him look at her with such indifference.

"You might as well say something, Sahara," Kyle said casually, leaning against the doorframe of their master bedroom. "Being quiet isn't going to make this go away."

Sahara looked at him in disbelief. She clutched a wrinkled piece of paper in her trembling hand. "What do you expect me to say? How am I supposed to take this? My God, Kyle. After all these years..." Tears rolled down her waffle-brown cheeks as she gazed incredulously at her husband.

Kyle looked at his wife and sighed. He hadn't wanted it to go down like this, but he almost felt it served her right for snooping through his things. "I don't know what you want me to say, Sahara."

Sahara gaped. "You could tell me why you decided to cheat on me with my own damn cousin, of all people!"

She waved the letter she had found in his gym bag that read of her husband's declarations of love and promises of forever to her first cousin, Wanda. She hadn't been snooping; she was looking for his car keys because she had accidentally left her organizer in his car the night before. The last thing she expected to find was a love letter from her husband to another woman. "If you were that unhappy, why didn't you just talk to me instead of running off with my *cousin*?"

"I've been trying to tell you for *months* that I wanted more out of this relationship. You've gotten boring and complacent; we never have any fun or do anything other than sit around the house and watch movies. I got tired of it." Kyle pushed himself off the doorframe and sauntered over to the mahogany dresser, where he emptied the change from his pockets into a small glass dish he kept there. "I admit I could've gone about it better than this, but you know Wanda and I had always hit it off. I actually met her first back in high school and we always had fun together. But when I saw her a few years ago at our class reunion, we just picked up where we left off."

Sahara's light brown eyes tightened at this information, all of which was new to her. "I never knew you were all that close."

"You knew I knew her, Sahara."

"Of course I knew you *knew* her; she was a bridesmaid in our wedding. But I certainly didn't know you were so tight or whatever. Damn it, Kyle!" she exclaimed, briefly dropping her head into her hands before looking back up at him. "How could you do this to me??"

Kyle sighed again and raised his hands. "I don't want any dramatic scenes, Sahara. Let's be adults about this. You knew I was unhappy."

"Then you divorce me, Kyle. You don't mess around with my cousin!"

She couldn't believe his whole attitude about this, like she was wrong for being upset about this. Like the fact that they weren't quite as happy as they once were was sufficient reason to commit adultery. He was going about his evening routine like none of this mattered in the least to him. Like their eight years of marriage and four-year old daughter meant nothing.

She glanced down at the crumpled letter in her hand. Words could not express how she felt when she read, in her husband's very own handwriting to Wanda, how he couldn't stop thinking about her and how they were going to be together very, very soon. It was apparent from the words he wrote that this had been going on for months. And right under Sahara's nose. She couldn't understand it; it's not like she worked a steady job. She just cleaned a few houses a week to get some pocket money. Kyle had always insisted on being the primary breadwinner. And when their daughter Rison was born, he insisted that Sahara quit her job as an account executive and be a full-time mother. She agreed because she loved her child and husband more than she loved her career. But it wasn't until now that she realized Kyle had probably been off cheating on her the whole time. She didn't even want to know exactly how long this had been going on, or if there were any other women.

Kyle paused for a moment before joining her on the bed. A part of him felt bad for what he was about to do, but a bigger part was actually waiting to exhale. "You're right, Sahara. That's exactly what I should have done."

It took a minute for his words to register. When they finally did, she looked at him, shocked. "What?"

Kyle's handsome face looked tensed when he said, "Please don't hate me. But I want a divorce."

CHAPTER ONE

E*ight months later*

• • • •

"THANK YOU, MRS. CHAPMAN. I appreciate that. You take care of yourself and I'll see you next week. And tell Marcus I said hello."

Sahara ended the call and entered the new appointment into her day planner that lay open across her small, moderately-cluttered desk. Her month was filling up quickly. Word had spread steadily about her cleaning business, *Clean Me Up!*, and now her once-in-a-while hobby had turned into an actual career. She was so proud of herself. Now she actually had something to fill her days and keep her mind occupied, aside from her daughter, of course. The past few months had been pretty close to hell on earth for her.

Kyle had served her with divorce papers mere days after admitting to his affair. She could only think that he had been planning to give them to her before she found that letter.

Now he was engaged to be married to the cousin he cheated on her with. Sahara couldn't believe it. After eight years of marriage, he just ended it like it was nothing. Sahara couldn't find one shred of evidence that showed he cared about how all of this was affecting her, or how it would affect their daughter. He was getting what he wanted, and that's all that mattered to him. It was all about him being *happy*. That's all. Sahara couldn't believe how cold and heartless he had been about the whole situation.

A bitter chuckle escaped from Sahara's lips when she thought of how Kyle had 'generously' offered to let her keep the house. But Sahara had refused, opting to get a nice apartment for her and her daughter instead after a brief period of staying with her mother to get her finances in order. She didn't want to have to deal with the memories that house contained or even entertain the notion that Kyle might have had her cousin or some other woman in their bed.

Thank goodness she'd had the good sense to put away money all these years. She'd grown sickeningly dependent on Kyle over the course of their marriage, but not completely so. She had her mother, Julia, to thank for that. Julia had divorced her husband of thirty years when Sahara was just a teenager, and Sahara remembered how she, her younger brother, and her mother had moved into a condominium across town immediately after the papers had been filed. Julia had told her daughter back then:

"Never ever put all your eggs in one basket, or all your faith in any man. Always keep something for yourself. 'cause nothing in this life is guaranteed."

Those words never rang true until she had actual divorce papers in her hand.

The fact that Kyle didn't seem to care about her at all anymore hurt Sahara to her core. She didn't do anything to deserve this kind of treatment. Kyle had been her one and only ever since high school; she hadn't even looked at another man. Any advances that were brought on by her long, shapely legs, creamed-coffee-colored eyes and dimpled smile were quickly spurned or politely ignored. She wanted the world to know that she was a happily married woman. Her mind, body, and soul had all been for Kyle, and she had no idea that his had been for somebody else. And her cousin, of all people. That's what hurt the most. Her cousin Wanda that had grown up with her, that had thrown her bachelorette party, that had stood beside her at her wedding, was now engaged to her ex-husband.

Sahara grabbed a handful of her full, shoulder-length raven tresses and forced herself not to cry for the thousandth time since Kyle had told her he wanted a divorce. *You have to get it together, girl*, she admonished herself. *Move on. Kyle has.*

She shuffled some papers on her desk and scanned her desk calendar to take note of her upcoming jobs. She was looking over some invoices when there was a light knock on her door. "Come in," she called out, still perusing the papers.

Her four-year-old daughter Rison timidly walked into her office. It was unbelievable how much she resembled Kyle and it still pained Sahara to look at her for too long sometimes. "Yes, sweetie, what is it?" Sahara asked her.

"Mommy, when is Daddy coming to get me? I'm ready to go to the park."

Sahara checked her watch. "He'll be here in a little while, baby. He's still at work."

Rison played with one of the thick braided ponytails that hung on either side of her head. "Will you come with us this time, Mommy? It's more fun when you come."

Sahara took a deep breath and tried to keep her composure. It still wasn't easy telling her child that her parents wouldn't be doing very many things with her at the same time anymore. It was hard enough trying to explain why they had to move out of their house and into this apartment without Kyle. She thought she did an okay job of explaining it, but she would have liked it if Kyle had been there to help her with that conversation. It was all happening because of him, but that didn't seem to matter. Sahara had tried to get him to come and help her explain things, but he never seemed to have the time. All he ever said was to tell Rison that he loved her and that he would be over to see her soon. He assured Sahara that she could handle that by herself. It amazed her that he could be so cavalier about something this important. It's not like Rison was an adult or even a teenager and could truly understand something of this magnitude. She was four years old, for goodness sakes.

But as usual, the only thing that mattered to Kyle was what Kyle wanted.

"Mommy has some work to do, sweetie, and plus Daddy wants to spend some time with you all by himself. You all are gonna go to the park and play, and if you're a good girl, maybe he'll take you to get some ice cream afterwards."

"Yayyy!" Rison cheered, jumping up and down. Her pigtails bounced around her adorable face.

Sahara smiled. She loved making her daughter happy, which was something she had to work overtime at since her and Kyle split up.

"I'm gonna go and watch cartoons until Daddy gets here. Okay, Mommy?"

"Okay, sweetie. Go ahead."

Rison ran out of the office. Sahara just looked after her and blew out a breath.

She wondered if she was up to the task of raising Rison as a single mother. It was a position she never thought she would be in, but here she was. No one could have told her that she and Kyle wouldn't be together forever, eventually having more kids and being the kind of family everyone else envied and patterned their own after. She used to see single mothers in the grocery store or in church or wherever and have such sympathy for them, but glad that she wasn't in their position. She had a husband who loved and provided for her and her child. Boy, was she fooled.

Nevertheless, Sahara knew that there was no way she was going to let Rison suffer in all of this. At least, not very much. Rison loved her father and still sometimes came home looking for him. She didn't really understand that when parents divorce, they stop living together. She always expected him to come back. Sahara always tried to explain that Kyle lived somewhere else now, but Rison would always come back with the impossible age-old question, "Why?"

That stumped Sahara because she wanted to be honest with her daughter, but she knew that there were some things that she couldn't tell her...like that her father had cheated on her mother with cousin Wanda and then decided to marry her, leaving Sahara high and dry. As true as it was, Sahara always wanted to avoid saying anything negative about Kyle in front of Rison and didn't want to give their daughter the impression that her father was a bad man.

Even if Sahara *did* think that he was being a cold, heartless bastard, there was no way she could tell Rison that.

Sahara checked her watch. Kyle was supposed to come get Rison at around four o'clock, which was in about another hour. Sahara continued to work at her desk, paying bills and whatnot, and tried to keep her mind off of Kyle. She was still not over him and probably wouldn't be for a while. He was the only man she had ever loved and it was hard to let that go.

But she knew she would have to suck it up and move on, as hard and as impossible as that seemed now. Kyle was already moving on to the next phase of his life, not thinking about her at all. Sahara had no idea what the next phase of *her* life would be. She didn't have a contingency plan for herself in case she and Kyle ever split up because she never thought it would happen. It wasn't *supposed* to happen. Thank goodness for her mother, though, who had been right there to help her with whatever, be it if it was just an ear if Sahara wanted to vent or a sympathetic shoulder when she wanted to cry. It was Julia who had encouraged her to go ahead and start her cleaning business full time, partly to help keep her mind off Kyle but mostly because she thought Sahara needed something for herself. Julia referred a few clients to Sahara as well as helping to go around handing out flyers and business cards just about everywhere they went. Sahara's business was really picking up and she was grateful to her mother for her hand in getting it started, and proud of herself for being able to maintain it.

When four o'clock rolled around, Kyle hadn't shown up. Sahara didn't think too much of it, figuring he was just running a little late or something. Rison came back into her office saying she was hungry, so Sahara went to fix her a little something to eat. At four-thirty, Kyle still hadn't shown up or called. Sahara tried to call him at his office and on his cell phone, but she got no answer on either. She just tried to keep Rison entertained and her mind off the fact that her Daddy still wasn't there. Sahara was just glad that Rison couldn't tell time yet.

At a quarter after five, Rison started getting antsy and asking for Kyle repeatedly. Sahara had no idea where he was. He still wasn't answering his phone and Sahara was upset. She knew he didn't forget that he was supposed to take Rison to the park today because she had just reminded him yesterday and had talked to him earlier that morning. He had said he was looking forward to it. And now he was nowhere to be found. Sahara hoped nothing had happened to him.

"Mommy, where's Daddy? I wanna go to the park now," Rison whined.

Sahara glanced at her watch again. "It looks like Daddy won't be able to make it, sweetheart. Why don't *I* take you to the park and then we can go get some of that ice cream? How does that sound?"

"Yayyy!" Rison cheered. She ran to get her jacket. Sahara was glad that all it took was a promise of ice cream to appease her but knew there would come a day when that wouldn't be enough.

While at the park, Sahara watched as Rison ran around, repeatedly going down the slide in between running around with a couple of other little kids and asking Sahara to push her on the swing. She was having a ball, seemingly forgetting about Kyle standing her up. Sahara hadn't forgotten, though, and knew Kyle had better have a very good reason for not showing up and not calling.

She tried to put that out of her mind for the time being, though, and just focus on her child, who was laughing and squealing loudly as some little boy playfully chased her. Sahara chuckled. She was just glad Rison was having a good time.

When it started to get dark out, Sahara rounded up Rison and they headed out to get ice cream like Sahara promised. After they were seated and were each digging into their cups of butter pecan, Rison asked out of the blue, "Mommy, how come Daddy lives somewhere else now?"

Sahara tried not to sigh out loud. She knew she had to be patient with Rison; she was only a child and still didn't understand what was going on, regardless of how many times Sahara had explained it to her. "Because Mommy and Daddy decided not to be together anymore, sweetie. Daddy went to live on his own, but he still loves you very much."

"How come he didn't want me to come live with him?"

"Because I wanted you to stay with me. It would break my heart if you and I didn't live together. But Daddy can come see you anytime he wants."

"Then how come he didn't come today?"

"I'm sure he wanted to but he was probably busy. He'll make it up to you, I'm sure."

"Okay," Rison finally said, scooping some more ice cream into her mouth.

Sahara was relieved to be done with this round of questioning, but was internally furious with Kyle for putting her in this position. She was the one having to deal with all these tough questions while he was off doing God knows what. It just wasn't fair.

Later that night, after Sahara had given Rison a bath, said her prayers with her and tucked her into bed, Sahara grabbed her new Connie Brisco novel and curled up on the couch. She was about ten pages in when her phone rang.

"Hello?"

"Sahara, its Kyle. Is Rison asleep?"

His voice still had an affect on her. "Of course she's asleep, Kyle. It's almost nine o'clock. What happened to you today? She was waiting on you."

"I know, and I'm sorry," Kyle said remorsefully. "One of my buddies was stranded on the side of the highway and he called me to help him. It ended up taking longer than I thought it would. I'm really just now getting home. You know how long those auto mechanics can be."

"You couldn't call? I tried to reach you a hundred times."

"You must've called after I had already left the office. My cell phone was dead since I had forgotten to charge it last night, and I didn't have my charger with me. I'm sorry about that."

"It's not me you need to be worried about. Rison is the one that's been asking for you all day."

Kyle sighed. "I hate that I disappointed my baby girl. I know she was looking forward to going to the park."

"Yes, she was. But I went ahead and took her."

"Oh, good. I'm glad she still got to go."

"Kyle..."

"I know, Sahara. I apologize. This will not become a habit."

"I hope not. Because I'm still having to field questions about why you don't live with us anymore and all that. It would be nice if you could help with that, seeing as how all of this is your doing."

"Sahara, look, just tell her I love her and I'll come and get her this weekend. All right?"

Sahara shook her head. That's what he always said. "Whatever, Kyle."

"I'm serious."

"All right." Sahara didn't want to argue.

"Okay, then. I'll talk to you later."

"Bye."

Sahara was still upset about Kyle standing Rison up but decided to give him the benefit of the doubt. She figured that something like what he said happened could have happened. There were plenty of times she was at the car mechanic's for hours when she hadn't planned to be. She still thought he could have called, though. There was a phone *somewhere* in that mechanic shop. Or he couldn't borrowed his friend's phone.

She tried to resume reading but her mind kept wandering back to Kyle. Despite herself, she missed him. She still wasn't completely used to sleeping alone at night. There was nothing like having someone to snuggle up to and she didn't like not having that anymore. Even if it was just for Rison's sake, she wished her and Kyle could get back together. Maybe it was foolish of her, but that's what she wanted. She wanted her husband back.

Across town, Kyle was snuggling up to Wanda on their chaise lounge in the den in front of the fireplace. He hugged her voluptuous body close to him and kissed her forehead. "Well, that's done," he said.

"Did she buy it?" Wanda asked.

"Yeah. Sahara's very trusting, almost to a fault sometimes. I figured she wouldn't ask too many questions."

"Good," Wanda said, smiling up at him.

"But I'm gonna let you know, Wanda; I don't like missing time with my child like that. It killed me, standing her up."

"I know, baby. But you and I have hardly spent any time together these past few days, with you working so much. We *needed* this quality time. Didn't you enjoy it?" she asked flirtatiously, placing a wet kiss on his neck.

"You know I did. But I don't like that my daughter is always asking where I am and then I don't show up, regardless of what the reason is. I'm not trying to be disappointing her like that."

"I understand. It was just this one time; I won't interfere on you all's time again."

"Good. 'Cause as much as I love you, baby, Rison has to come first. The divorce is rough enough on her as it is. I don't want her thinking I left her as well as her mother."

"I know."

"I just want us to be on the same page," Kyle said, leaning down and giving her a peck on the lips. He leaned his head back and closed his eyes.

Wanda hugged Kyle around his waist as she rested her head on his chest. She didn't feel sorry in the least for convincing Kyle to stay home with her instead of going to see Rison. They needed their quality time together. Rison would always be his daughter but until she had that ring on her finger, Wanda was dispensable. She didn't want to give Kyle any pause about making her his wife.

And besides, Wanda didn't really care for Rison. It wasn't that she disliked her personally, she just disliked that she was Kyle's daughter with another woman. That meant that there would always be someone that would come before her. So Wanda felt she had to do what she had to do, seductively enticing Kyle into spending a romantic evening at home instead of going to some park. By the time she was finished with him, he couldn't have gotten up and gone anywhere if he wanted to. She did her best to wear him out.

Kyle had no idea that Wanda really didn't like kids and had no plans of having any of her own, even though she had led Kyle to believe otherwise. He had it in his mind that he was gonna knock her up with three or four children, but he just didn't know. Wanda had been willing to tell him whatever he had wanted to hear in order to get him to leave Sahara for her. It wasn't like Sahara couldn't have had any more kids, but it was just like the cherry on top of the sundae.

Wanda was spontaneous and fun and sexual and uninhibited, and she had a body that Kyle had never been able to keep his eyes off of, even during his marriage to Sahara. After they reconnected and started hanging out more, Wanda decided to make it her mission to make Kyle hers. And if that meant letting Kyle think that she wanted to give him a houseful of babies, then so be it.

He'd find out after they were married, though, that her getting pregnant at *any* time just wasn't going to happen.

CHAPTER TWO

"You want some more pot pie?" Julia asked, getting up to get herself some more lemonade. "I made plenty."

"No, I couldn't eat another bite," Sahara responded, wiping her mouth with her napkin. She pushed her plate away. "But thanks, though. It was delicious."

"Glad you like it. 'Cause I'm sending some home with you."

Sahara chuckled. "All right."

She watched as her mother filled a big Tupperware container with the remaining chicken pot pie and then wrapped up a huge hunk of the German chocolate cake she baked. It was Sahara's favorite. Julia was always doting on Sahara and Rison and Sahara would be lying to herself if she tried to say she hated it. She loved that she and her mother were so close and she hoped that she and Rison would have that kind of relationship.

After Julia finished packing the bag of things to send home with her daughter and granddaughter, which ended up including more than just the pot pie and the cake, she rejoined Sahara at the table. Rison was in the living room watching the Spongebob Squarepants DVD that Julia had gotten for her.

"So, how are you two holding up?" Julia asked.

"Rison is okay, I think. She still asks her questions but she seems happy. I, on the other hand, still find myself missing Kyle."

Julia's eyebrows shot up. "Really?"

"Yes. Maybe I shouldn't, but I want him back. I just get so lonely, Ma; I never, ever would've thought that I would be getting a divorce, for *any* reason."

Julia looked at her daughter sympathetically and reached over to rub her hand. "I know, baby. I've been there. Getting used to being alone after having been married can be tough, and when there are children involved, it's a whole 'nother story."

Sahara nodded and looked thoughtfully down at the ground. After a few moments, she looked at her mother and asked, "Do you think I'm stupid for wanting him back after what he did to me?"

"Of course not, baby. You're human. And when you're in love, you're willing to overlook a lot of things. Love is powerful and can make you accept things you otherwise wouldn't. But just remember that even if you and Kyle *did* get back together, it still wouldn't solve your problems. You were lonely and having trouble before you found out about Wanda."

"Yeah, that's true," Sahara admitted sadly.

"This is a tough time for you, and it hurts me to watch you go through it. But you can. And you'll be a stronger person because of it. Just focus on Rison and growing your business and take getting over Kyle one day at a time. It gets easier, trust me."

Sahara smiled at her mother and squeezed her hand, thankful to have her. This had to be the toughest time of her life and she didn't know if she would be able to get through it as well as she was if it wasn't for her mother in her corner, giving her encouragement. Julia had been through all of this herself so she knew what Sahara was going through, although Sahara thought that Julia had handled it much better than she seemed to be. Julia never seemed like she missed her ex-husband, and if she did, she did an award-worthy job of hiding it. Sahara just wasn't that good of an actress.

Ever since she met Kyle during her sophomore year of high school, he had her. They didn't even begin seriously dating until their junior year, but Sahara always had a feeling that they would end up together. She loved how he seemed to have all of his stuff together; he had a five, ten and twenty year plan and knew exactly how he wanted to go about working it.

That wasn't at all common among the rest of the boys that tried to step to Sahara. They only cared about what was in the moment and having fun. And while there was nothing wrong with having fun, Sahara had never been the typical teenager who loved partying and going out and dating a lot of guys at once; she had always been an old soul, thinking about finding a husband before she was even legally able to marry him. And when she met Kyle, she knew he was it. There was just something about him that spoke to her and she wanted to know what else there was to him. He was handsome but he was considered somewhat of a nerd, which seemed to turn off most girls but it intrigued Sahara. Intelligence was very attractive to her. After they started dating, they would go to the library or to one of their parents' houses and do their homework together before they did anything else. Seeing how Kyle breezed through everything only inspired Sahara to work harder on her own studies. She started getting the best grades of her life after being with Kyle only one semester, and she just knew that it was sign that they were right for each other.

College was tough because they didn't go to the same school, and Sahara really put a lot of effort into making sure they kept in contact with each other regularly. She never even thought about getting with anybody else. After they finally graduated, Kyle seemed to really appreciate how Sahara had stuck by him and he proposed to her after he got his first job in his field. Sahara couldn't have been happier. She vowed to be the best possible wife she could be to him. And she tried.

But somewhere along the way, they seemed to start venturing down different paths and wanting different things. Kyle started wanting to go out more and try new things, which Sahara wasn't exactly opposed to but she just was more of a homebody. She looked forward to going home after a long day and just snuggling up with her husband instead of going back out somewhere. Kyle felt that he had spent years focusing on his studies and establishing himself, and now that he had done that, he wanted to have more fun when his work days ended. Sahara just wanted her and Kyle to close themselves off from the rest of the world after they each got home.

Clearly wanting different things, the marriage started to unravel, but Sahara didn't see it until it was done. All their years together or the fact that they had a child couldn't put it back together, apparently. Kyle wanted out and Sahara couldn't beg him anymore to stay.

While at church the next Sunday, Sahara listened intently to the fervent message of the preacher to hold on to God's unchanging hand. She found comfort in that word *unchanging*. That meant He wouldn't switch up the program and get bored with her and cast her out. She squeezed her eyes shut and rocked side to side, praying for strength to get through this trying time in her life, and to be the best mother she could be to her daughter Rison. It was a struggle sometimes to remember she had a child looking up to her and that she had to remain strong, even when she wasn't feeling it on the inside.

Sahara was glad she went to church because she had honestly been thinking about *not* going since Kyle still attended there. Thankfully, though, she hadn't run into him. It was a big congregation so it wasn't that hard to get lost in the crowd. She knew seeing him would only reignite her yearning for him and she was trying to get past that.

After the service, people were milling around, shaking hands and hugging and fellowshipping, and Sahara noticed a woman she hadn't seen before. Even though it was a sizeable congregation, Sahara always tried to make an effort to at least remember everybody's faces, and she had never seen this woman's before.

She must be a visitor, Sahara thought to herself, walking towards her.

Approaching her, she smiled warmly. "How are you today? I'm Sahara Johnson."

The pretty woman smiled brightly and shook Sahara's offered hand. "It's nice to meet you! I'm Charlie Stephens."

"Are you a visitor?"

"I'm actually a new member. I just joined last Sunday."

Sahara had missed that Sunday because Rison was sick. "Oh, okay, great. Well, welcome! I hope you find that you're happy here. This is a wonderful church to be a part of."

"Yeah, I can tell. Everyone's been great to me, and Pastor Roy is amazing."

"Isn't he? His messages always manage to touch my spirit. Are you new to the city?"

"In a way. I haven't lived here since I was four years old so it's just like I am. So much has changed."

"Oh yeah. Things are different than they were just two years ago so I can imagine," Sahara replied. "You wanna sit down?"

"Sure."

They sat down on one of the pews and talked for another twenty minutes or so. Sahara really liked Charlie. She was sweet and they seemed to really hit it off, realizing they were on the same page about a lot of things. Sahara never really had any close friends and she hoped that Charlie could develop that kind of relationship, especially since Charlie said she didn't know that many people in town. They exchanged numbers, promising to get together soon. Sahara was already looking forward to it.

Before she left, Sahara stopped to talk to Pastor Roy for a few minutes. She loved that he was always willing to talk to his members, even though he had so many of them.

"Pastor Roy, thank you so much for the Word today. It was great," Sahara praised.

"Well thank you, Sister Johnson. I hope something I said today helped you."

"It most certainly did. As always, it seemed like you were speaking directly to me."

Pastor Roy smiled. "That's conviction. That's always a good thing." He took a step closer to her. "I know you're going through a rough time right now. I'm praying for you and if you ever need to talk, just call. All right?"

Sahara smiled. "Thank you so much, Pastor. I appreciate that."

"All right, Sister. And say hello to your mother for me."

Sahara started to head towards the nursery to get Rison so they could leave. She wanted to go ahead and get started on the pork chops she had thawing at home because Rison was always hungry right after church.

She happened to look up and see Kyle and Wanda in the back of the sanctuary, laughing and talking with another couple. Kyle had his arm around Wanda's waist and would occasionally lean down and kiss her on the forehead. Wanda was leaning into him, making it clear he was hers. They looked so happy together and Sahara actually threatened herself not to cry. She couldn't help being hurt; she was nowhere *near* the point where she could see them together and it not affect her. It had only been a few months.

Turning quickly, she hurried out of the sanctuary before she lost it, not wanting them to see her.

Once she and Rison were on their way home, Sahara wondered if she would ever get over Kyle. It had been eight months and she didn't seem to be making any progress towards it. She still wished that he would come to his senses and come back to her, and she would be more than willing to forgive him.

But deep down, she knew that probably wasn't going to happen. Kyle and Wanda had looked so happy earlier, like they were already married, even. Sahara hoped that they would just start going to another church so she wouldn't risk running into them as much, because who knew when she would get used to seeing them together like that. Kyle didn't even go down to the nursery and see Rison before he left. Rison wouldn't have been able to stop talking about it if he had. Sahara guessed he had been too busy socializing and hugging up on Wanda to go and visit with his child.

Sahara blushed when her thoughts wandered to the night before when she was rolling around in her cold bed, sweating and sexually frustrated. She hadn't been with anybody since Kyle, and truth be told, she had never been with anybody *before* Kyle, either. He had been her first and only. And the nights when she missed having him to make love to where becoming more and more frequent. She would writhe around in her bed, stuffing pillows between her legs and trying her best to pretend that they were Kyle's body. Of course, that never worked. She wanted *him*. She wanted to be kissed and touched and caressed by *him*. And it burned her up that he was somewhere doing to Wanda what she wanted him to do to her.

This wasn't how it was supposed to be. He was supposed to keep his vows to her and be there when her body wanted or needed some attention. She had never really tried to pleasure herself, and the thought of going out and getting someone else never entered her mind; that wasn't her style and she wouldn't feel right bringing some strange man to the apartment she kept her child in. Sahara never thought much about casual sex, probably because she had never had to. She always had Kyle. But now...she didn't. And she knew she was going to have to do a better job of handling it.

CHAPTER THREE

"Hey Wanda, I'm about to head out to get Rison. I'll be back in a few hours, okay?" Kyle called out, picking up his keys from the end table in the living room.

"Okay. Oh, can you come back here for a minute before you leave?" Wanda called from the bedroom.

"I'm running late, baby. What do you need?"

"I need you to come back here. It'll only take a minute."

Kyle sighed, looking at his watch. He was supposed to take Rison to the aquarium and he should have left to get her ten minutes ago. He had been doing some work from home and he lost track of time. He rushed around the house getting ready, and now that he was almost out of the door, Wanda wanted something.

"This had better be good," he mumbled to himself as he stalked back towards their bedroom.

He opened the door and his eyes widened. Wanda was sprawled across the bed wearing nothing but a white g-string and some red pumps. She arched her back when Kyle entered the room so her breasts jutted forward, inviting him to move closer. Kyle licked his lips but resisted the urge to go over to her.

"Ahh, baby...what's going on?" he croaked, his throat suddenly dry.

"I wanted to show you what I picked up today," Wanda purred, eyeing him seductively. She reached out to him. "Come get a better look."

Kyle hesitated. "I have to go, Wanda."

Wanda pouted. "Please? I just want you to feel the material. Its very *soft*," she teased, running her fingers down the thin piece of fabric that covered her womanhood.

Kyle grunted at the image of Wanda touching herself. He wanted nothing more than to go and rip that flimsy undergarment from her body, but he had been looking forward to seeing Rison all day. Sahara had already called and told him that Rison was over there all ready to go. He could just picture his baby girl repeatedly looking out of the window and asking Sahara when he was going to get there. The image made him want to hurry up and get to her.

"Wanda...can you just hold that thought until I get back? I really...*really* have to get out of here," Kyle said, his body already responding to the erotic image of his fiancée.

"Hold that thought? What, you think I'm supposed to just lay here for hours while you go and look at fish with your daughter? Come on, honey...she can wait a little while longer. The aquarium won't close 'til later tonight. Just come and play with me for a little bit before you head out."

Kyle weakened. Wanda could see it and decided to go in for the kill. She got up on her knees and ripped off the g-string, then stepped off the bed and sauntered over to him wearing nothing but the red pumps. Kyle's eyes roamed over her milk chocolaty body that was thick in all the right places, and his mouth actually started to water. His hand reached out to touch Wanda's hips as she stepped close to him and started licking his neck, which always drove him crazy. Her body pressed against his and Kyle couldn't help but wrap his arms around her. When she looked up at him with her thick-lashed bedroom eyes reminiscent of Loretta Devine, he couldn't help but lean down and kiss her. He moaned when her tongue eased into his mouth and she backed him into the wall behind him, unbuckling his belt. He gave in to her when she dropped down to her knees, pulling his pants with her.

A couple of hours later, he was on the phone with Sahara, trying to explain himself. He told her that a pipe had burst in the house right as he was getting ready to leave and he had to call a plumber. He knew Sahara didn't know anything about that kind of stuff and would just have to take his word for it. It was clear that she was upset, though, and she told him that Rison had cried when Kyle never showed up. He felt incredibly guilty; he had never liked to see his baby girl cry. This had to be the last time he stood her up because he didn't want her to start thinking he was trying to abandon her.

Kyle couldn't explain it, but Wanda had some kind of incredible hold on him. All she had to do was turn on the sultry voice or bat those eyes at him and he was weak in the knees. He loved her so much and found that he wasn't very good and denying her the things she wanted. Making her happy made him happy.

He couldn't wait to marry her and for them to start their own family. Two more kids would be perfect, and it would be great if one of them was a boy. And when the time was right, he planned on getting custody of Rison. That was something he hadn't told anyone but Wanda, but he wanted it. He felt like he could take care of and provide for Rison much better than Sahara could, seeing as how he was a partner in a major architectural firm and Sahara just had a small cleaning business with herself as the only employee. It wasn't that she wasn't a good mother; Kyle just thought he could be the better father.

Of course, he hadn't been doing a good job of proving that as of yet. Wanda wanted him all to herself and didn't seem to like the idea of sharing him with anyone, even his own child. Once she got used to Rison being in the picture more, she would stop being so clingy and they could all be a big happy family. Kyle was sure of it.

Wanda laid in their king-sized bed, listening to Kyle lie to Sahara again on the phone as he paced up and down the hallway in front of the bedroom. She had distracted him on purpose and didn't feel guilty about it. Kyle was *her* man now and Sahara and Rison were just going to have to get used to that. They couldn't be expecting Kyle to be running over there every time they needed some attention. Things had changed and they needed to get with the new program.

While they were making love, Kyle had asked Wanda if she wanted to go ahead and start trying to get pregnant. He said doing it now wouldn't matter since they were planning on getting married, anyway. Wanda told him she was on the pill, which wasn't true, but it didn't matter. She wouldn't be getting pregnant, not now or at any time in the future.

And Kyle's little plan of getting custody of Rison wasn't going to happen, either. She wasn't sure how she was going to go about it, but she was going to put a stop to that whole scheme. She would let him *think* that she was supportive and behind him one hundred percent, but after that ring was on her finger, all the pretending would stop and he would learn what the real deal is and the way it was going to be.

Rison was Kyle's daughter and she wasn't going anywhere; Wanda would just have to live with that. But that didn't mean that she wanted her to move in with them so she would be expected to baby-sit and bond and monitor herself around the brat. No, this was *her* house. Wanda felt like this was her and Kyle's time to be together and she didn't want anyone getting in the way of that, not even his own daughter. Let Sahara keep her.

There was only a small, small part of Wanda that felt guilty for breaking up Kyle and Sahara's marriage. Too small to really even acknowledge. She had simply been the better woman for Kyle and he would've been a fool not to do something about that. Wanda had to admit she had always been jealous of Sahara when they were growing up because Sahara was so effortlessly beautiful and didn't even realize it. She had physical gifts that she didn't even know how to use. Wanda thought that was such a waste.

But seeing as how Sahara had always been such a goody-two-shoes, she wouldn't do anything, anyway. Wanda was willing to bet that Kyle had taken Sahara's virginity. Sahara always used to talk about how she wanted to wait until she was married to have sex with someone (or *make love* as she used to call it) so that meant that she didn't lose her virginity until she was twenty-three. There was no *way* Wanda could have done that. Her cherry had been popped in her early teens. That gave her worlds more experience between the sheets, and now Kyle was finally getting the benefit of it twenty-four-seven. Sahara might have had the better body and the beauty, but Wanda had the moves that seduced her husband into her bed and kept him there.

Wanda found some pleasure in shattering Sahara's perfect little life she had built. Saving herself for her high school sweetheart, graduating from college, *marrying* her high school sweetheart, having his baby, and quitting her job to be a stay-at-home mother. All of it made Wanda sick to her stomach and she just wanted to throw some paint on the pretty picture. Why should Sahara get to be the one who got to sit at home all day while her man brought home all the bacon? Wanda felt like *she* deserved to be able to do that. Kyle made more than enough to support her and she wanted to be the one who didn't have to work. And as soon as they were married, she was quitting her nursing job. Kyle didn't know that either, though. She smiled as she buried her head in her goose-down pillow, imagining herself in the good life of being Mrs. Kyle Johnson.

In the meantime, Kyle was on the phone again with the former Mrs. Johnson, listening to her fuss at him for standing their child up again. She said that she ended up having to cancel on a client at the last minute because she didn't have anybody to watch Rison. Kyle felt bad about that because he knew that cancelling appointments wasn't good for business, and if nothing else, he wanted Sahara to succeed so she could take sufficient care of Rison until she came to live with him.

"I sincerely apologize, Sahara," Kyle said, leaning against the wall in his office. "It's not like I'm trying to be a jerk here. I told you what happened."

"Yeah, Kyle, but try explaining that to Rison. She's just a child. She doesn't care anything about your pipes bursting or whatever. All she knows is that her daddy didn't show up when he said he would *again* and she was crushed."

"This wasn't expected, Sahara. It was really last minute."

"Of course, it always is. But you're not the one that has to see the look of disappointment on her face when she realizes you're not coming, or console her as she cries, asking how come you don't love her anymore."

Kyle's heart sank. "She really said that?"

"Yes, she said it. I wouldn't make something like that up."

Kyle knew that. He knew the kind of person Sahara was and knew she wouldn't say something like that unless it was true, especially since it was about their daughter. It just hurt Kyle to his heart that Rison would ever think that he didn't love her. He knew it was his own fault for putting Wanda's needs ahead of his own child's. But that was going to stop.

"I promise you, Sahara, this will *not* happen again," Kyle said emphatically.

"I hope not."

Wanda, who had gotten up to get something to drink from the kitchen and had stopped at the doorway to the office to listen when she heard him on the phone with Sahara, smirked to herself.

We'll just see about that, she thought to herself.

CHAPTER FOUR

O ne Saturday afternoon, Sahara invited Charlie over for lunch. They had begun talking almost daily since they met at church a couple of weeks prior and Sahara felt like she was really gaining a close friend. It did a little towards filling the void she felt after Kyle left.

Rison was spending the day at Julia's, so Sahara and Charlie had a good time having girl talk and laughing loudly about things. Charlie already adored Sahara and couldn't imagine why someone would want to leave her the way Kyle did. Sahara had confided in Charlie about that, telling her all about her and Kyle's history and everything about how she was doing he left her. It felt good to Sahara to spill her guts like that to someone. Telling her mother was one thing, but confiding in a girlfriend was another.

"I am so sorry you had to go through all that," Charlie said sincerely as they sat down on Sahara's couch. She took a sip of her tea before putting it down on a coaster on the coffee table. "Do you feel like you're handling it better than you were at first?"

"Only marginally," Sahara replied. "It's still hard for me to think about how things used to be, and it kills me to see him with Wanda. I guess I'm just amazed that he can already be so happy with somebody else so soon after leaving me. I'm still a wreck."

"You were blind-sighted, honey. Kyle had been messing around with that woman for months before you ever found out about it. It'll take some time but you'll move past this."

"I'm glad you think so 'cause I'm really not seeing it right now."

Charlie smiled and reached over to squeeze Sahara's shoulder. "Trust me, it will. Just keep praying and focusing on that beautiful daughter of yours. Remember God never gives us more than we can handle. You're stronger than you think you are."

"Hmph. To be honest with you, girl...I don't really *want* to be strong right now. I mean, I know I need to be for Rison's sake, but when it comes to Kyle...I can't help but miss him. He was the only man I had ever loved or shared myself with. I couldn't say that if he showed up here right now saying he wanted me back that I wouldn't go."

"I understand, girl, believe me I do. You gave your heart and soul to that man for years and then he pulled the rug out from under you. It takes time to get over that. It hasn't even been a year yet. You'll get there, though. I'm here for you and I hope you know you have my support for whatever you need."

Sahara smiled at Charlie gratefully. "I can't tell you how much I appreciate that, thank you. It's always good to know someone has your back."

"Definitely. But in the meantime, Sahara, have you ever given any thought to dating again?"

Sahara looked genuinely surprised. "No, not really. That's never even crossed my mind. I'm still hung up on Kyle."

"While I do understand where you're coming from on that, you have to remember that Kyle is the one who cheated on *you* and then left you for your cousin, not to mention how he keeps standing Rison up. Do you *really* want to be with a man like that?"

Sahara never thought about it like that. When she put it that way, Kyle *didn't* come out sounding all that desirable. But it didn't change the fact that he was the man she was still in love with. She was sure that the way he was acting now was because of Wanda. She was a bad influence on him.

"He didn't used to be like that. He was always so good to me. If things could just go back to how they were before..."

"But they can't," Charlie said gently, placing her hand over Sahara's on the couch. "We can't go back, we just have to move forward. And as difficult as it may be to admit, Kyle is moving forward with Wanda. You have to do the same."

"I don't know if I can, though, Charlie. I am *so* out of practice. Kyle is really and truly all I know. He was my first boyfriend, first love, first lov*er*, first everything. Part of me has been hoping he'll come to his senses and come back to me, and I can't say that the whole reason for that is me missing him. I wouldn't have to worry about trying to get out into the dating game. I honestly have no clue what to do when it comes to that."

"Girl, you are a beautiful woman. I bet there are all kinds of men who would give their right arm to go out with you."

"If there are, I don't know anything about them."

"Kyle had your nose open so much, you weren't paying attention to anybody else. But it's a new day and its time for a new attitude. Finding you someone to go out with shouldn't be any kind of problem. I can introduce you to some people, if you want. There are some really cute guys at my job."

Sahara bit her lip nervously. She had to admit she was a tiny bit intrigued at the idea of getting out and dating. Maybe it would break up the monotony that her life had become.

Outside of Rison, Sahara had been feeling like she was just going through the motions. She would go to work, pick Rison up from school, spend the evening with her before bathing her and putting her to bed, and then spend the rest of the night pretending to read or get some work done but ended up doing more thinking about Kyle than anything else. She felt helplessly pathetic and maybe meeting somebody new was just the thing she needed. Charlie had been right when she said that Kyle was moving forward. While he was moving forward, Sahara was standing still, cemented to the spot she was in when he left her in his dust. It was time to take a step.

"I guess I can give that a try," she said timidly.

"Great!" Charlie exclaimed happily. She clapped her hands and Sahara chuckled. "You are going to feel so much better about yourself, mark my words."

Sahara sure hoped so. Because with every lonely night that passed, she missed the company of a man more and more. Physically, emotionally...in *every* way. She was only slightly embarrassed to admit that she was constantly aroused and had recently begun to explore masturbation. It was either that or pull her hair out from the sexual frustration. It amazed her how good she could make herself feel, but knew that it would be even better with a man.

Not that she would jump into anything sexual immediately after beginning to date someone, but eventually things would get to a physical level. And while she still wasn't sure where she stood on the whole casual sex issue and didn't know if she wanted to wait until she was married again before she gave her body to another man, she took solace in that they didn't necessarily have to have sex for her to receive pleasure. Because as she was learning, there were parts of her body that could make her orgasm just as good if they were treated right.

Charlie stayed over for most of the afternoon before she left. Julia dropped Rison off early in the evening, and she and Sahara played for a while before Sahara gave her a bath and then put her to bed. Sahara just stood there looking at her sleeping child for a while, thanking God for her and again praying for the strength and wisdom to be the kind of mother Rison deserved. If nothing else, Sahara was thankful she got a beautiful daughter out of her failed marriage.

After cleaning up the kitchen and straightening up some more around the apartment, Sahara decided to get ready for bed. She took a warm shower and then slipped into her favorite nightshirt. It was actually an old basketball jersey of Kyle's that fell just above her mid-thigh. She liked to wear it because it made her still feel connected to him.

Just as Sahara was climbing into bed, she heard a knock on her front door. Frowning, she glanced at the clock on her nightstand. It was almost eleven. She couldn't imagine who would be showing up at her door out of the blue like this. She walked cautiously towards the living room, stopping briefly to peek in on Rison, and wondered if Charlie had sent her first dating prospect over. But she dismissed the thought, knowing Charlie wouldn't send a strange man to her house this time of night, and with Rison there.

Sahara hoped there was nothing wrong when she tiptoed to the front door and called out, "Who is it?"

"It's Kyle."

"Kyle?" Sahara said, releasing the chain and cracking open the door. She peered at Kyle standing out on her front step. "What's going on? What are you doing here?"

"Can I come in?"

Sahara hesitated. What could he possibly want? She slowly opened the door the rest of the way and let him in, curiosity getting the best of her.

"I came to see Rison," Kyle said once he was inside. "Where is she?"

"What do you mean, where is she? It's after eleven o'clock. She's asleep."

"Well, can you wake her up? I really want to see her."

Sahara couldn't believe his nerve. "I am not waking that child up because you decided to come over here out of the blue. Maybe you wouldn't miss her so much if you'd quit flaking on her. And just so you know, I don't appreciate you coming over here this time of night and unannounced. I have a phone. You could've called first."

"Look, I'm sorry about that. But I was working late and thought I'd stop by on the way home."

"You were working at this time of night on a Saturday?"

"I have a big project coming up. It requires a lot of overtime."

Sahara remembered all those times she was alone in the house because he had been working late. Some of those times, he was probably with Wanda, too. That thought just occurred to her. "Well, be that as it may, you're just gonna have to come back at a more decent hour. She's not supposed to adjust to *your* schedule, Kyle; you have to make time for *her*."

"It's not like it's gonna take that long, Sahara. Just let me go in and see her right quick," Kyle said, heading towards Rison's bedroom. Sahara rushed to stop him before he opened the door. Rison wasn't the heaviest sleeper and Kyle wouldn't be the one who would have to get her back to sleep if she woke up. He'd just play with her for a while and then go home.

"Leave her alone, Kyle," Sahara said, putting her hand over his to stop him from opening the door. She gently pushed him back towards the living room. "As I said, you're going to have to come back another time."

Kyle sighed as Sahara pushed away from Rison's room. He hated that she was mere feet from him and he still wouldn't get to see her. Maybe it *was* little late to just be stopping by, but he honestly didn't think Sahara would mind. It's not like he was coming over for a booty call or something.

Although when he looked at Sahara in that old jersey of his, he couldn't help but notice how good she looked. It didn't look like she was wearing a bra and he could see flashes of her cleavage through the large armholes. And she still had the prettiest legs he had ever seen. They were long, shapely, and soft. Sahara always had the softest skin he ever felt on a woman.

She smelled good, too; like she had just taken a shower. Kyle knew she was oblivious to how enticing she was. She was extremely modest and unaware of the effect her looks had on people; always had been. He always liked that about her. Usually women who looked as good as her did all they could to flaunt it or make others feel bad for not looking like them. Sahara was never like that. She was a genuinely sweet woman. Kyle hated that things had to turn out the way they did between them.

Sahara was admiring Kyle, too, although a little more subtly. She was still very much attracted to him and seeing him standing in front of her in his casual slacks, polo shirt and jacket made her want to go to him, wrap her arms around his waist, and inhale whatever cologne it was that he was wearing. He looked good and she felt her body responding to the sight of him. She tried to will it to stop, but it was futile. She wanted him. She wanted him to stay there with her and not go back to Wanda.

"Well...I guess I should be going, then," Kyle said after a few moments of silence. He tore his eyes away from his ex-wife's body and turned towards the door. "I'll call you about when I can come get Rison." He opened the front door.

"Kyle," Sahara called out quickly, partly because she didn't want him to go and partly because she had the sudden urge to ask him the burning question:

"Why did you do me like you did? Why did you cheat on me with my cousin?"

CHAPTER FIVE

Kyle sighed and looked down at the ground, wondering if he had the energy to get into this. As much as he didn't want to go there, he knew Sahara deserved some kind of explanation.

He closed to door and turned around to face Sahara, who was standing a few feet away from him with an anxious look on her face. It looked like she really wanted, or needed, for him to answer her question.

"Come on; let's sit down," he said, heading towards the couch. He sat on one end as Sahara sat on the other, facing him. She waited patiently while he tried to gather his thoughts and find the right words.

"Sahara...I never planned on things turning out the way they did. I really did love you and I have to say a part of me still does. You're a good woman. But it's like I told you before; I just got bored. We never did anything exciting or varied from the same routine that we seemed to have fallen into. I just felt like something was missing. As much as I tried to get you to vary, you just seemed comfortable and I couldn't see myself going through the rest of my life like that. Maybe that's just the way you are, but it didn't go well with the way I was anymore."

Sahara looked like she was hurt but trying not to show it. "Well...you couldn't find a better way to handle it than to do what you did? I mean...she's my *cousin*, Kyle."

"I know," he said, actually feeling kind of guilty for the first time. "As I said, I never planned it this way. Wanda had a lot of the things I liked in a woman even back in high school, but you were the one I fell in love with. Then she and I lost touch, and you and I were doing so well. I honestly never really thought about her. Then when I saw her again at that reunion, it brought something back to me...I can't really explain it. All I knew was that I didn't want to lose touch with her again. So we exchanged numbers. Then we started hanging out, having lunch together or meeting for a drink after work. Then one night she invited me over for dinner and it just..." His voice trailed off, not really wanting to say it. He figured Sahara could figure out the rest.

A tear ran down Sahara's face as she looked down at her hands. She didn't want him to see her crying. She had told herself that she wasn't going to cry over Kyle anymore. But hearing him go into detail about what went down with Wanda, which apparently had been happening right underneath her nose, she just couldn't help it. Hearing that she wasn't good enough for him hurt her. Even though it wasn't really news to her anymore and it had been months since she had initially found the letter that changed everything, it still hurt.

Kyle had always hated making Sahara cry. He hesitantly reached for her hand and inched a little closer to her on the couch. "Sahara...whether or not you believe it, it doesn't make me feel good to see you like this."

"Really?" She sniffed, looking at him.

"Of course." He paused, wondering if he should tell her what he was thinking. Figuring he might as well be honest and get everything out in the open, he forged ahead. "Sahara, I think it's only fair to let you know that Wanda and I are planning to have our own family one day. Now, I know I haven't been the best father to Rison lately, but I want her to be a part of everything." He conveniently left out the part about planning to take custody of Rison once he and Wanda were married.

Sahara looked surprised. It really never occurred to her that Kyle and Wanda might want children of their own one day. That would mean they were really moving forward and even if for whatever reason their marriage didn't work out, they would still have that child together. If nothing else, at least Sahara could say she had Kyle's child. Wanda couldn't say that, at least not now. But if they had children in the future, then Sahara wouldn't have any leg up at all.

"Well...um, I don't really know what to say to that, Kyle."

"I just wanted to be honest with you. Look, you and I are gonna have to deal with each other pretty much indefinitely so I really hope that we can learn to get along. And not just for Rison's sake...we've got too much history behind us to not be more than just cordial towards each other."

Sahara's face brightened, somehow finding hope in Kyle's words. "Maybe we can be more than that, Kyle. I mean...you said you still love me so...why don't we give us another try?"

Kyle sighed. "Sahara..."

"No, Kyle, really," Sahara pleaded desperately, scooting closer to him and clutching his arm. "I can change...I can be more fun and spontaneous and whatever else you feel it is you need!"

"It's not that simple, Sahara-"

"But it *can* be, Kyle! You and I were good together, plus we have a daughter! Just think about that; we're gonna be linked together for the rest of our lives, plus like you said, we have a *lot* of history. You don't just throw all that away! Please Kyle..."

Kyle looked at her pained face and had to look away. She looked so desperate...he didn't want to be callous but he had to let her know that what she was asking of him simply couldn't happen.

He turned to her and grabbed her hands in his, searching for the right words. She looked at him eagerly.

"Sahara, look...I don't want to hurt you. I really don't. But...I...you and I are through. I'm with Wanda now. I'll always be there for our daughter but you and I can't happen again."

Tears cascaded down Sahara's face. "Kyle..."

"Daddy?" Rison said in a groggy voice, emerging from her bedroom and rubbing her eyes. She squinted, adjusting her eyes to the light.

"There's my baby girl!" Kyle exclaimed, happy to see his daughter and relieved to be freed from the awkward situation Sahara had just put him in. He released her hands and stood. Sahara turned away from Rison, wiping her tears and trying to compose herself.

"Daddy!" Rison happily ran to her father, grinning. Kyle scooped her up and swung her around a few times, causing Rison to laugh and squeal.

As the two of them spent time together, Sahara tried to get herself together. She couldn't believe that she had let herself lose control like that. After all these months and the progress she was finally starting to make getting *over* Kyle, all it took was a few kind words from him to cause her to make a complete fool out of herself and beg him to take her back. How humiliating.

And now on top of everything else, she would have to look him in the eye, knowing he would remember this. Not to mention, he would probably go and tell Wanda about it and they would have a good laugh at her expense. So now not only had her cousin taken her husband, now Sahara had gone and begged him to take her back and he turned her down flat. When was she going to learn?

"I have to go now, baby girl, but I'm gonna come and get you this weekend, all right?" Kyle told Rison.

"Can we go to the park, Daddy?"

"We can do whatever you want, baby."

"Yayyyy!" Rison cheered, jumping up and down.

Kyle smiled and kissed her on the cheek. "I'll see you then, baby girl." He looked at Sahara, who didn't seem to want to look at him. He could tell she was embarrassed, but he didn't know what to do or say to put her at ease, especially in front of Rison. So he just said, "I'll talk to you later, Sahara. Good night." Then he left.

"Did you hear that, Mommy? Daddy said we could go to the park!" Rison exclaimed.

"Yes, I heard, sweetie."

"Will he get me some ice cream, too?"

"I'm sure he will," Sahara said, standing up. "Now you go on and get back in the bed. It's too late for you to be up."

"All right. Good night, Mommy. Can you tuck me in again?"

Sahara smiled. "Sure, I can. Come on."

A couple of days later, Sahara was still kicking herself for begging Kyle to take her back like she did. Every time she thought about it, it made her squeeze her eyes shut in embarrassment. There was no way she could tell Charlie or her mother about it. They wouldn't laugh in her face but there wouldn't be any way to tell what they were thinking, and Sahara couldn't bear wondering what would be going through their minds about her.

As hard as it was to accept, she knew that things were really and truly over with Kyle. It was time to start putting sincere effort into moving on. Sure, she had been holding on to the hope that he still had some feelings for her; they had been together a long time and she would like to think that he wouldn't just forget about all that. But apparently even if he hadn't, it wasn't enough to keep him with her. It wasn't enough to make him leave her cousin alone.

Speaking of her cousin, Sahara hadn't spoken to Wanda in months. It certainly wasn't because she hadn't seen her; they went to the same church and they occasionally saw each other around town. They just never spoke. Sahara really didn't know what to say to her. She knew she was *supposed* to forgive her cousin, but it wasn't the easiest thing to do. Wanda had slept with her husband and taken him from her, leaving Sahara to be a divorced single mother. While Wanda certainly wasn't the only one to blame in all this, Sahara just wasn't able to bring herself to fully forgive her yet. She knew it would take a while, and she really wasn't in any hurry.

One thing that kind of puzzled Sahara, though, was several memories from their childhood where Wanda had expressed rather adamant disinterest in ever having kids. She used to say that she didn't want to have to take care of anybody for eighteen years other than herself. Sahara mused that it must have just been the rantings of a selfish child, because she had apparently changed her mind. Kyle was certainly handsome enough to make any woman want to make babies with him.

Either that, or Wanda just wanted to have a baby out of spite to rub it in her face. It would be a mean and spiteful thing to do, but Sahara knew better than to put anything past her cousin.

And while she would never will anything negative upon an innocent child, Sahara couldn't help wishing that the baby between Kyle and Wanda never be born.

CHAPTER SIX

"You've got to be kidding me," Julia said, astonished.

"I wish I was," Sahara responded.

"I can't believe Kyle stood my baby up again. She must be crushed."

"Yeah, she is. She ran to her room crying when it became obvious that Kyle wasn't coming. I offered to take her to the park and out for pizza but she didn't want to go."

"Oh," Julia groaned painfully, her heart hurting at that image of her granddaughter. She always liked Kyle all right, but she could just strangle him for the way he had been treating Rison lately. His leaving Sahara for her cousin was bad enough. But constantly disappointing his child was simply inexcusable. "So where is she now? Is she feeling any better?"

"A little. I just gave her some dinner and now she's in her room playing."

"Didn't you have an appointment tonight?"

"Yeah, I did. But since Kyle never showed up, I had to postpone it so I could stay here with Rison."

"Why didn't you call me, Sahara? You don't need to keep missing these appointments. This is your business and how you support yourself and your child."

"I know, Mama, but I couldn't leave Rison like that."

"I understand." Julia sighed. She adjusted the phone between her ear and shoulder as she stuffed dirty clothes into her washing machine. She closed the lid and leaned down to retrieve the freshly dried clothes from the dryer. "But the next time this happens, bring her over here. I don't want you to ruin your business because Kyle won't act right."

"Mama-"

"Don't even argue with me, Sahara. I told you I was here to help you with Rison whenever you needed me to and I meant it. So if Kyle stands that child up again, you just bring her right over here with me and I'll take care of her while you go to work. You hear?"

Sahara smiled. She loved her mother so much. "Yes, ma'am. Thank you."

Sahara would never forget the image of her daughter's face as it crumpled when Sahara had to tell her that it didn't look like her father was going to make it. She didn't want to lie to Rison and make up some kind of excuse, but she actually didn't even know what the truth was since Kyle still hadn't bothered to call. She surely hoped he was all right and that nothing had happened to him, but she figured he was probably caught up doing his own thing and not even thinking about what he had told his child, *again*. He didn't even have enough consideration to call this time.

Kyle never used to be like this. His family used to always come first. But ever since he divorced her and moved in with Wanda, things had changed drastically. He didn't spend nearly enough time with Rison and even his child support had decreased a little bit, no doubt thanks to Wanda's influence. If there was anything Sahara knew about her cousin it was that she was selfish. She didn't like to share her Jolly Ranchers on the playground back in the day and she probably didn't like sharing Kyle's time and resources now. It didn't matter that Rison was his daughter and only four years old; Wanda didn't like to share *as* a child and she didn't like to share *with* a child. That was just the way she was.

Sahara hoped, though, that she was mistaken. That maybe there was a legitimately good reason why Kyle hadn't shown up for Rison yet again. And maybe Wanda had nothing to do with those reasons. He could very well be stuck at work or stuck in traffic or stuck beneath the mangled wreckage of his totaled car, which would be an example of a good reason for him not calling. It could be anything.

Besides, Sahara and Wanda hadn't been close in years. People change. She could be a completely different person than Sahara remembered. It was certainly possible. And it was better to think that way than to think that she was deliberately trying to keep Kyle away from Rison. Sahara dismissed that thought, deciding it was ridiculous and choosing to think positively. Her hurt and embarrassment were obviously causing her imagination to run wild.

After Sahara finished talking to her mother, she decided to go to her office to get some work done. She was checking her emails when Rison appeared in the doorway.

"Mommy?"

"Hmm?"

"How come Daddy don't like us anymore?"

Sahara's head snapped towards her daughter. "What? Why would you think something like that?"

"He never comes to take me to the park or his house anymore. Is he mad at me?"

Sahara's heart hurt. "Oh, sweetie...come here," she said, reaching out to her. Rison walked over to her and climbed into her lap, laying her head against her chest. Sahara held her child close to her as she searched for the right words. "Your daddy loves you just as much as he always has. He just has a lot going on right now. I'm sure he really wishes he could be with you right this second."

"Where is he?"

"Um...I'm not sure, sweetie. But I'm sure he'll call you soon."

"If he calls tonight, can we go to the park then?"

"It's kind of late to go to the park now. But maybe he'll come and see you for a little while." As soon as that was out of her mouth, Sahara wished she could take it back. She didn't want to get Rison's hopes up for nothing. Lord knows Kyle did enough of that.

"I hope so. I miss Daddy."

Sahara closed her eyes and tried to compose herself. She absolutely hated to see her baby hurting like this. "I know you do, baby. But please don't think that your daddy doesn't love you. He loves you very much and so do I. All right?"

"Okay."

Sahara kissed her on the forehead and patted her back. "Go on back in the living room and play while Mommy finishes up some things. I'll be in there in a little bit."

Rison slid off of Sahara's lap and ran back into the living room.

Sahara sighed as she looked after her daughter. She replayed Rison's questions in her mind and felt herself becoming angry. She simply could not believe Kyle's nerve. His neglectful behavior was now causing Rison to repeatedly doubt his love for her, and he needed to know about that. Sahara was sure she would have heard from him by now, but since she hadn't, she would just have to call him. She needed to know what was going on.

She dialed his number and listened to the song that played as the phone rang, silently reminding herself to keep her cool when she heard Kyle's voice. Because at the moment, she was thinking about using words she just really didn't like to use.

Her rehearsed speech went out the window, though, when she heard a woman's voice answer the phone instead of Kyle. "Hello?"

Sahara was momentarily stumped. She wasn't prepared to talk to Wanda. "Hello, Wanda. It's Sahara."

"I know who it is, silly girl. You're my cousin! What's up?"

Sahara rolled her eyes. Wanda was talking like they were best friends or something. "I was actually trying to get in touch with Kyle. It's really important. Are you anywhere near him?"

"I'm not, actually. He ran out to the store and forgot his phone. Anything I can help you with?"

"Umm..." Sahara debated on whether or not she wanted to get into this with Wanda. Whether or not she was about to be Kyle's wife, she didn't know if she would ever get used to discussing issues about her and Kyle's child with her. It just didn't seem right. "Kyle never showed up to get Rison today and he never called. I was wondering what happened."

"Girl, you lying! He had told me about his plans with Rison and when he went out today, I was *sure* that's where he was going! And you say he never even called, huh?"

"No, he didn't."

"Hmph. Well, I'll tell you what. As soon as he gets back here, I'm gonna get to the bottom of this. There is just no reason for that. I bet Rison was really disappointed, too, wasn't she?"

"Very. She ran to her room crying."

"Oh, bless her heart. I apologize, girl. But best you believe, I will be getting in his ass as soon as he walks in the door."

Sahara blushed but smiled. Wanda actually sounded upset about this. Maybe she *had* changed and wasn't as bad as she thought, after all.

"Thanks, Wanda. I appreciate it. When you're done with him, can you please have him give me a call?"

"I sure will. Go kiss that baby for me and I'll talk to you later," Wanda said sweetly before she hung up the phone. She wanted to laugh out loud at how incredibly gullible her cousin still was. Sahara would believe anything. Some things never change.

Ever since they were kids, Wanda knew she could get over on Sahara whenever she chose to. She was nice and trusting to a fault. She had this naïve, Nickelodeon thing going on where she wanted to see the good in everybody, even if deep down she knew there wasn't much there. Wanda chuckled to herself. *Sahara had actually believed I gave a damn about Kyle standing that little girl up again*, she thought to herself, adjusting her bathrobe around her body. *If I have it my way, this won't be the last time, either.*

Kyle came out of the bathroom, still slightly wet from his shower. "Did I hear my phone ring?"

"Nope. You must have water in your ears or something," Wanda teased.

Kyle smirked. "Yeah, okay. I could've sworn I heard it. Anyway, how are you feeling? Any better?"

"A little bit. I still need you to nurse me back to health, though. Why don't you go get your stethoscope so we can play doctor?"

"Baby, chill out with that. You're sick."

"You know you always make me feel better."

Kyle just shook his head and smiled, drying the back of his neck with the peach towel that was draped over his shoulder. He went back into the bathroom and Wanda smiled to herself. She had "suddenly" come down with something when Kyle was getting ready to leave that morning. He was going to go into the office for a few hours before going to get Rison, so she picked that time to come down with her mysterious virus so as not to look to obvious by waiting until right before he was supposed to go see his daughter. She put on such a good performance that Kyle had nothing on his mind but making her feel more comfortable and easing her pain. She knew he hated to see her not feeling well and there was no way he would leave her alone like that. He worked for a while in his home office while Wanda feigned weakness and stomach pains and dizziness. Every now and then he would come and check on her, but for the most part he was in his office. That was fine with her. At least he was in the same house with her and not out with Rison or anywhere around Sahara. And in the meantime, she got a day off from work and her wishes catered to.

And speaking of work, Wanda had been on a mission to convince Kyle that she should quit her job. Sahara had been a stay-at-home mother, having quit their job after she got pregnant. Wanda felt like she should be entitled to the same privilege, but she wasn't trying to wait until she started pretending to get pregnant or even until they were married. She wanted to do it *now*. Her job as a registered nurse was more stress than she needed in her life. She had a man that made more than enough to take care of her comfortably, so why shouldn't he? That way, she could be home waiting for him everyday in a different color thong and those red pumps he liked for her to wear so much.

"Baby," she called out.

"Yeah."

"Can we talk about the job issue?"

"What about it?" he asked, emerging from the bathroom again.

"What about it? You know what I'm talking about, Kyle. I want to go ahead and quit my job. We're already living together. I don't see what there is to wait for."

"I would simply just like for us to hold off on that until we get married. Which would be a lot easier if you would be willing to set a date, but you keep putting it off. That's not my fault."

"But, baby, I *hate* my job," Wanda whined, leaning slightly towards him on the bed. "Don't you want me to be happy?"

"You know I do, but-"

"Just think of all the things I'd be available to do for you if I didn't have to worry about working twelve-hour shifts three days a week. I could have dinner ready for you when you get home from those long days, draw your baths, be rested up for those long, marathon lovemaking sessions that I sometimes don't have the energy for now..."

"Wanda, we've discussed this. Now you know I hate seeing you unhappy in any way, but this is something I just want to wait on. All right?"

Wanda pouted, looking up at him through her long eyelashes. "Fine."

He picked up his watch from the dresser and bit his lip. "You know, it's not all that late. Maybe I can still go and see Rison."

"You can't do that," Wanda blurted out.

He looked at her, surprised. "Why not?"

"Um, I'm still sick, Kyle. You gonna leave me here all by myself?"

"You're a grown woman, Wanda, and a nurse on top of that. I'm sure you can take care of yourself for a couple of hours."

Wanda reached for him and he automatically stepped closer to her. She ran her hand up and down his thigh as she rolled over onto her side, her bathrobe falling open to reveal her bare breasts. "Well...can you lay that beautiful body on top of mine for a while before you go? Just for a few minutes. I could use the body heat." She eyed him seductively.

Kyle's eyes strayed to her exposed breasts and he felt his body responding to her. She was looking at him with those eyes that always made him forget everything else, and before he knew it he was opening her robe and laying down on top of her, enjoying the feeling of his skin against hers. She clamped her legs around him and wrapped her arms around his neck, purring softly in his ear. A smirk came to her face as she felt him getting hard underneath her and she knew he wouldn't be going anywhere. He couldn't resist her.

"You're temperature is going down," Kyle murmured, grazing his lips up and down her neck.

Wanda had placed Lye soap underneath her armpits to raise her body temperature as well as placing an extremely hot towel over her face and neck. Kyle didn't even bother taking her temperature; he heard her say that she wasn't feeling well and that was good enough for him.

"You can help bring it back up," she whispered naughtily.

"Mmm..." Kyle moaned. He licked her collarbone snuggled closer to her. "You're a bad girl."

"If only you knew," she said, lightly biting his earlobe. "But you know you like it."

"Yes I do."

They laid there all hugged up, teasing and licking each other occasionally and whispering dirty things into each other's ears. After a while, Kyle tried to push himself off of Wanda's writhing body.

"Where do you think you're going?" she asked.

"I'm going to go see Rison before it gets too late. I don't want Sahara to get too upset with me. I can't not show up again and I'm already hours late as it is."

Doesn't he know Sahara's name is not welcome in this bed? Wanda thought to herself. *And who cares if she got upset? Certainly not me.* "Okay, but I have something to tell you before you go."

"What?"

She stuck her tongue into his ear and pushed her hips up harder against his. "I'm ready to set a date."

Kyle grinned. "Yeah?"

"Yeah. Let's celebrate. Get a condom."

CHAPTER SEVEN

Sahara put the finishing touches on Ms. Ericson's upstairs bathroom and began gathering her supplies. She had just finished cleaning her third house of the day and she was just ready to get home and collapse onto the couch.

"I'm all done, Ms. Ericson," Sahara said as she came back down the stairs. The older woman was sitting on her freshly fluffed couch, doing a crossword puzzle. "If you want, I'll wait so you can go and check everything to make sure it's to your satisfaction."

"Oh, I'm not worried about that. You always do a good job. Come, sit down here for a minute," the older woman instructed, patting the cushion next to her.

Sahara gladly took a seat on the slightly worn couch, resisting the urge to lay back and close her eyes. She was dog tired.

Ms. Ericson put her book down. "Sahara, baby, I've been wanting to talk to you about something. Now, you know I think the world of you and I think you are way too beautiful to be by yourself. When are you going to start dating again?"

Sahara's mouth fell open but she clamped it shut. For a few seconds she was actually rendered speechless. She hadn't seen that question coming. "Umm...I really don't know, to tell you the truth. I've just been focusing on Rison and my business..."

"And that's all well and good but that business isn't going to keep you warm at night."

Sahara's face flamed with embarrassment, not believing she was having this conversation. Ms. Ericson was like another mother to her, having been one of Julia's closest friends for years. It was Julia who had referred Sahara to her.

"Yeah, well...um..."

"I'm embarrassing you, aren't I? I don't mean to, baby. But I just don't want you to feel like you have to stay by yourself."

"I really don't-"

"Let me get right to it. I have someone I want to introduce you to. And just consider it before you say no," she added quickly, when Sahara opened her mouth to do just that. She wasn't comfortable with being set up, especially by one of her mother's friends. What if she decided to go out with this guy and ended up hating him? How would she handle that?

"Here's his picture," Ms. Ericson said, reaching for a photo album underneath one of the end tables. She flipped it open and handed it to Sahara, pointing to a picture on the first page. "That's my nephew, Jacob. Now you can't say he ain't handsome."

Sahara had to admit that he was, in fact, *very* handsome. It was a pleasant surprise because she had been expecting the worst. "No, I can't," she admitted.

"See there? You need to meet him. He's a really nice boy; well-mannered, raised right. You all would have a good time together."

Sahara bit her lip as she continued to peruse the photograph. She couldn't deny that she was mildly interested. But still..."I'm sure he's wonderful, Ms. Ericson, but it's been a long time since I've dated anyone..."

"Baby, it's going to be even longer if you don't go ahead and start doing it now. I know you probably still have feelings for your ex-husband but its just not healthy for you to be alone so much without the company of a nice young man. What do you really have to lose?"

Sahara could think of a few things, like her time, her dignity, her pride...but at the same time, she *did* want to step out of her shell a little bit. There was nothing wrong with going on a casual date. And she was sure Ms. Ericson wouldn't set her up with someone unless he was a good guy.

"All right," Sahara conceded. "Give him one of my cards and tell him to give me a call."

"Perfect!" Ms. Ericson exclaimed happily. "He'll be calling you soon. I just know you two are going to hit it off!"

Sahara smiled, but her hopes weren't as high as Ms. Ericson's seemed to be. She just hoped she liked the guy enough to be able to tolerate an evening with him.

On her way home, Sahara wondered if she should be dating any more handsome men. Kyle was handsome and look what he had done to her. Maybe she should explore men who were less attractive physically, but she knew that she couldn't change what she liked just because she was scared of getting her heart broken.

And she had never been all about looks, anyway. With Kyle, it was his intellect that attracted her; the fact that he was so handsome was a bonus. But she couldn't lie and say that she didn't care about how a man looked *at all*. That's why this Jacob guy had intrigued her so much. He had this smooth-looking caramel skin, with thick eyebrows and dark wavy hair. There was a boyish quality about him that really attracted Sahara. The more she thought about it, the more she looked forward to meeting him.

A couple of nights later while out with Charlie, the subject of men came up again. They were out to dinner, with Charlie sipping on wine and Sahara nursing a glass of cranberry juice, when Charlie asked, "So, girl, have you thought any more about our conversation about you meeting some men? You haven't changed your mind, have you?"

Sahara put down her glass. "No, I haven't. Actually, one of my clients wants to set me up with her nephew."

"Yeah?" Charlie asked, looking intrigued. "Did she show you a picture or something or is it a blind date?"

"No, I think I have to draw the line at blind dates. She did show me a picture and I'm actually looking forward to meeting him."

"That's great! So I guess he looked good, huh?"

"Yeah, he did. I just hope it wasn't an old picture or something. It would be just my luck."

"Oh girl, stop. Quit thinking so negative. I'm glad you have a prospect. Have you talked to him yet?"

"No, not yet."

"Well, I'm sure he'll call soon. And when he does, I want you to go for it. But in the meantime, I have a couple of other dudes in mind I want to introduce you to. It's always good to have options."

Sahara's eyebrows shot up. "How many men do you expect me to go out with, Charlie? Dating a bunch of men at once has never been my thing."

"How do you know? Have you ever done it?"

"Well, no..."

"It's not like you have to sleep with them or anything like that, unless you just want to. But it's always good to have more than one option just in case your client's nephew doesn't work out. All you have to do is meet them. You might find that you don't like them, or they for whatever reason may not like you. Just roll with it, girl, and have a good time!"

Sahara blushed, but she didn't hate what Charlie was saying. There was something slightly...*naughty* about the idea of dating multiple men at once. It was something she had never even considered. Before she met Kyle, she was just thinking about getting that one boyfriend. After she met Kyle, it was just all about Kyle. He was all she needed. And now that Kyle was out of the picture, maybe she should shake things up. What could it hurt?

Nevertheless, she wondered if she could even maintain something like that. She didn't even know what the rules were. Was she supposed to tell these men that they weren't the only one she was seeing or keep it to herself? How long was she supposed to wait before she brought them around Rison? She didn't know what a respectable amount of time was. Was she supposed to wait until she was in love? She didn't want to bring just anyone around her daughter, or let her see a string of men coming in and out. And what about if Rison went and said something to Kyle about the men she dated? What would happen then? Not that he could do anything about it; she was free to date if she wanted to and he certainly wasn't in the position to give her any grief about that.

"Do you still think about Kyle?" Charlie asked gently, as if reading her mind.

Sahara played with her napkin. "At times."

"It's only natural. You won't get over him overnight. But I just think that you're way too good of a woman to be pining over a man like Kyle. Life goes on."

"True."

"Tell you what. How 'bout you meet me and a couple of guys out on the town one night. Then you don't even have to worry about meeting anyone on your own; you just show up and try to have a good time. What do you think?"

"I don't know, Charlie..."

"What's not to know? There's no pressure. You don't have to get married. It's just a night on the town with your girl, her guy and his friend. Just a little double date. You could stand to have some fun, right?"

Sahara couldn't argue with that. Between all the drama with Kyle, running her business and still getting adjusted to being a single mother, she hadn't had much time for fun or even really realized she was without it. When she really thought about it, her entire life had been pretty reserved and devoid of fun. She was still young; barely in her thirties. There was no reason she should be spending most of her evenings in her apartment with nothing but the company of her daughter, work, and a few good books and movies to keep herself entertained.

"Yes, I could," Sahara stated confidently.

"All right then. So you just let me know what night is good for you and then we'll make it happen."

"Great!"

Their entrees arrived and they began to eat. After a few minutes, Sahara's cell phone vibrated in her purse. She fished it out and groaned when she glanced at the number.

"What's wrong?" Charlie asked.

Sahara held up a finger as she answered the call. "Yes, Kyle?"

"Sahara, I just wanted to apologize for the other day. What happened was-"

"Kyle, I really don't want to hear it."

"I know you're upset and you should be, but I have a really good reason-"

"Save it. There is *no* good reason for continuously disappointing your child and lying to her *and* to me over and over. So whatever your excuse is this time, just keep it to yourself."

"Sahara-"

"I'm busy, Kyle. I'm gonna have to talk to you later."

"Well, can I at least speak to Rison right quick?"

"No, you cannot."

"Why not?"

"Because she's not here. I'm out right now."

"Out?" Kyle asked, shocked and immediately curious. "Out where?"

"Well, not that it's any of your business, out with my friend Charlie."

Kyle paused. That was the last thing he expected to hear. He immediately wanted to know more. "Charlie, huh? What, you out on a date or something?"

"Why do you care?"

"I don't. I mean, I do but I don't. I...I just didn't know you were dating...so soon."

"I have to go, Kyle."

"Sahara, wait! I mean...so where'd you meet him?"

Sahara wanted to laugh out loud. She realized what this was all about. Kyle thought Charlie was a man and he actually sounded jealous. *Well, it serves him right*, she thought to herself. *Let him sweat a little bit.*

"I'll talk to you whenever, Kyle. I'm being rude to my date over here," Sahara said, winking at Charlie. Charlie stifled a giggle, putting a hand over her mouth.

"Hold up a second-"

"Bye, Kyle." Sahara ended the call and tossed it back into her purse, laughing along with Charlie. "Can you believe him?"

"Face it, girl," Charlie said, sticking her fork into a piece of her steak, "Sounds like you've got a jealous ex-husband on your hands."

CHAPTER EIGHT

Kyle didn't know what to think.

He just couldn't believe that Sahara was dating already. He never heard her mention anyone named Charlie so she must have met him since they split up, and he couldn't help wondering where they met. She never used to be in the habit of going out a lot. What, now all of a sudden she was going out on the town and stuff? Around his daughter? Where was Rison when she was going out meeting all these men?

As hard as it was to believe, Kyle found himself not liking the idea of Sahara dating. He couldn't explain why. He knew he didn't have any claim to her anymore, nor did he even have the right to be upset about anything she did. She was a good woman, a beautiful woman; he had said so himself. It was only natural that some other men start taking notice. Maybe it was arrogant of him, but he honestly never expected there to be anyone else after him. Regardless of his already being engaged to another woman, he thought Sahara would just raise their child and work on building her business and be satisfied with that. It was a little unrealistic, now that he thought about it. It was only natural that after a while she would begin wanting to start seeing people. Almost a year had gone by since he left her. Most women wouldn't have waited this long.

But Kyle still didn't like it.

There were times when he thought about what he did to Sahara and felt guilty. He couldn't deny that it was wrong, having an affair with her cousin and then getting engaged to her before he and Sahara were even divorced. Sahara didn't

65

deserve that, and he knew it. The night he went to see Rison and Sahara begged him to take her back, the look in her eyes still haunted him. The hope and desperation and, after he told her he was staying with Wanda, the raw hurt and despair. He wished it didn't have to go down like that but he couldn't lie to her or lead her to believe that there was a chance for them when there wasn't. He obviously still had feelings for Sahara and in a perfect world, he would go back to her and try to make things work for the sake of Rison, but he just couldn't do it. He was madly in love with Wanda and he couldn't pretend otherwise.

Speaking of Wanda, he was beginning to think that she didn't want him to see his daughter. As ridiculous and far-fetched as it sounded, it seemed like every time he got ready to go and see Rison, she always found some way to keep him from going. It could very well be a coincidence but something in his gut was telling him that it wasn't. Her mouth was saying that she supported Kyle keeping a close relationship with Rison, but her actions were preventing him from actually doing it. When he confronted her about it, though, she adamantly denied it.

"Nothing could be further from the truth, baby," she had insisted, grabbing him around the waist. "You know I'm all for you spending as much time with that precious little girl as possible."

"That's what I thought, Wanda, but it seems like every time I'm about to go see her, you need me for something or find some way to convince me to stay with you. It's happened too many times in a row for me to just dismiss it as a coincidence."

"So, what, you think I'm doing that on purpose? Baby, you don't think any more of me than that? I knew when I got with you that you had a child and that she would have to come first. I can't help it if I happen to need you or something comes up when you're getting ready to go see her. And it's not like I had to twist your arm too hard to keep you from going."

Kyle couldn't even protest that because he knew she was right. He could have, and *should* have, put his foot down when Wanda tried to get him to stay. It was as much his fault as it was hers. Then he always ended up lying to Sahara about why he didn't show up. And besides, what reason would Wanda have to keep him from seeing his daughter? From what she always told him, she loved kids and supported his relationship with Rison. She was looking forward to being a stepmother and eventually a mother of their own children. It was possible that it *could* just be a coincidence, how things had been happening. It had to be. The woman he loved would never intentionally do something like that.

A couple of his friends had asked him why in the world he left Sahara for Wanda. Sahara was clearly the better looking of the two, not to mention having the better attitude. He could admit that sometimes Wanda could be a little abrasive and smart-mouthed. And she sometimes engaged in talking about people behind their backs, something Sahara never did. Sahara always tried to find something nice to say about anyone. Kyle knew she was one of the most kind-hearted people he had ever met.

But there was a certain intrigue to Wanda that he couldn't resist. She was spontaneous; he never knew what to expect from her and he liked that. She kept him on his toes and he never found himself bored with her. Even back in high school, they always had a good time together, tripping out about whatever and sharing a comfort level that he never quite achieved with Sahara. They were buddies as well as lovers. And on top of everything else, Wanda's body was *banging*. She was good and thick and he liked that. She knew how to use that body to make him weak in the knees every time. Their sex together was amazing. Once he had slept with her that night she invited him over for dinner, he was hooked. He just couldn't see giving that up. That's not to say the sex was bad with Sahara, but it was just twice as good with Wanda. He knew Wanda had more experience and it showed. He had been Sahara's only lover. Part of him couldn't help but wonder if he still held that title.

He tried to push Sahara and this Charlie guy out of his mind, but he couldn't help wonder who he was. Part of him wanted to call her and grill her about him, but he knew he had no right to do that. He wondered if she had taken him around Rison yet and how Rison liked him. Were they all doing things together, like a family? Kyle couldn't imagine Rison calling another man 'daddy.' Regardless of how he had been slacking lately, he was still Rison's one and only father and he didn't want either one of them to forget it.

He decided to drop by Sahara's and see his daughter. It had been too long since he had seen her and he missed her like crazy, and part of him had to admit he was hoping this guy Charlie was there so he could get a look at him. He didn't mention it to Wanda so there wouldn't be any chance of her hindering him. He just headed straight over there after working a few extra hours at the office. It was getting a little late and he knew Sahara didn't like him just dropping by, but she would just have to get over it. All he wanted to do was see his daughter...and possibly Sahara's new man.

When he turned on to Sahara's street, he started looking for her car. It was there in its usual space, and the lights were off inside her apartment.

They can't be asleep already, he thought to himself. *Maybe she's just back in her room.* He went over what he would say when she got onto him for stopping by unannounced. It was just a little after eight o'clock so it wasn't *that* late; she shouldn't have any problem with him seeing Rison for a little while. Just then he saw a car pull into the space next to Sahara's. Kyle stopped his car down the street and turned off the engine and the lights. He figured that was her date dropping her off and he wanted to see who the guy was. He ignored the little voice in his head asking him why he even cared.

He saw Sahara climb out of the passenger's side, looking beautiful with her hair pinned in a tousled off-center low bun and a black wrap dress that clung to her body. She had a smile on her face, like she had just been laughing about something. Kyle hadn't seen her so happy in a while. His eyes focused on the driver's side, waiting for this man she had gone out with to reveal himself. Thanks to the tinted windows on the car and the distance at which he had parked, he couldn't make out anything from where he was sitting. His eyes narrowed as the door opened and this Charlie guy got ready to make his appearance.

Kyle was shocked to see a woman emerge from the car. She was tall, with her hair slicked back in a high bun, and she had what looked like a dancer's body. He watched as she met Sahara on her side of the car and they stood there talking for a couple of minutes, laughing and occasionally touching each other on the arm or the shoulder. Then they hugged for what seemed like a long time to Kyle, holding each other a little too intimately, before kissing each other on the cheek. The woman got back into her car to leave and Sahara went inside her apartment, the smile still on her face.

"Well, I'll be damned," Kyle muttered to himself, sitting back in his seat. He replayed what he had just seen in his mind a couple of times before he re-started his car. He forgot all about his plan to see Rison as he pulled away from the curb and sped off a little faster than necessary. Of all the things he could have driven Sahara to, he never thought lesbianism would be one of them.

CHAPTER NINE

"**S**o you and Kyle are officially divorced?"

"Yep. We're officially divorced. I didn't try to contest it."

"And you shouldn't have. I never liked the bastard."

"Colin..."

"No, I'm serious, Sahara. There was always something about him that wasn't right to me. It was like he had something to hide. Looks like I was right."

"Is this some kind of 'I told you so'? 'Cause I don't really need to hear it if it is."

"Of course not, sis," Colin said, softening. "I just hate anybody mistreating my sister. And with cousin Wanda, of all people..." He whistled. "I never liked her, either."

Sahara chuckled. "I know you're just saying that to make me feel better."

"Is it working?"

"Of course it is."

Sahara was glad to talk to her little brother. They didn't get to talk as much as she liked because he was in the doctorate program at UCLA and he spent most of his time studying. They usually kept in touch via text or instant messenger; it was a rare treat when they got to talk on the phone.

Colin wasn't lying when he said he had never liked Kyle. Ever since Sahara got with him back in high school, he just tolerated him for his sister's sake since she was obviously so smitten with him, but he never spent much time with him himself or made any effort to really get to know him. Even after all their years together, he never grew to care for Kyle very much. In all honesty, he kind of saw this whole adultery thing coming. He never thought it would be with their own cousin, but when Julia had called him to tell him that Kyle had left Sahara, he was furious, though not surprised. If he was surprised about anything, it was that it had taken so long.

"Do you need anything, sis? I have a little free time coming up; I can come down there and handle him, if you want. I'm probably twice his size now."

Sahara laughed. "I don't doubt it. What are you, like 6'7 now?"

"Something like that. Close to three hundred pounds, too."

"Geesh. No wonder I always feel weird calling you my *little* brother. What the heck are you eating over there?"

"Please. With my schedule, I hardly have time to eat like I should. Thank God for Mama's care packages or I'd be living off of jelly sandwiches and cheese crackers."

"How nourishing."

"But seriously, do you want me to come and take care of that ex-husband of yours? I wouldn't mind at all, especially after hearing how he's been treating my niece."

"That's very comforting, Colin, but it's not necessary. We're fine. I'm not focusing on Kyle as much as I used to. In face, I'm about to get back into the dating game."

"Oh yeah? It's about time!"

Sahara laughed. Then she heard a beep, indicating that she had another call. She told Colin to hold and then clicked over to her other line. "Hello?"

"May I speak to Sahara please?" an unfamiliar male voice asked.

"This is she. Who's this?" she asked pleasantly.

"This is Jacob."

"Oh!" Sahara's heart pace immediately quickened. She was instantly nervous but tried not to let it show. "How are you?"

"I'm good. I've been wanting to call you for the past week or so but I've had a lot going on. My aunt told me she was gonna put a switch on me if I didn't call you soon."

Sahara giggled. That sounded like Ms. Ericson. "Well it's good to finally talk to you. I had to admit I was wondering if you were ever going to call."

"Oh, most definitely. I've been looking forward to meeting you. I know this might seem a little hasty and short notice, but I was wondering if you would be open to meeting up tonight."

"Tonight?" Sahara bit her lip. She was glad that he couldn't see her blushing.

"If it's too soon, I understand-"

"I'd love to," Sahara blurted out. After hearing his voice, she realized just then just how anxious she was to meet him and really begin the process of getting on with her life. "What time and where?"

"Do you like seafood? There's a new place over by Auntie's that I've been wanting to check out."

"I think I know the place you're talking about. That sounds great. Is seven-thirty okay?"

"That's perfect. So I'll...meet you there?"

"Sure. See you then." She grinned to herself as she hung up the phone. It immediately rang back and she remembered she had Colin on the other line. She quickly hit the TALK button. "Sorry about that, Colin!"

"Yeah, right! Geesh, I haven't talked to you in over a month and then you forget I'm on the phone? What kind of love is that?"

"Oh hush. That was Jacob, the guy Ms. Ericson was trying to set me up with. He asked me out; we're meeting up later on."

"Go 'head then, sis! I'm glad to hear that. Just be careful, all right?"

"I will. Now let me get off this phone so I can get some things together. I have to get someone to watch Rison tonight."

"Dang, now you're getting off the phone with me, too? Man. I hope this dude is worth it," Colin joked.

"Aww, you. I love you and I'll talk to you later, okay?"

"All right, sis. Love you, too."

Sahara hurried to her bedroom to try to find something to wear for her date that evening. She wasn't supposed to meet Jacob for hours but she couldn't help feeling a little anxiously excited. This would be her first date with anyone other than Kyle. And maybe it was a little premature, but she already liked Jacob. His demeanor was appealing to her.

But before she got herself all riled up, she needed to find a babysitter for Rison or else there would *be* no date.

Remembering how empathetic Wanda had been the last time they had talked, she called Kyle first. She thought that maybe he or Wanda could watch Rison. Wanda had seemed really upset with Kyle when he stood Rison up that time and Sahara hoped that would translate into her not minding watching her future stepdaughter for a few hours. Sahara had never allowed herself to think of Wanda being a stepmother to her daughter but she couldn't deny that it was an inevitable that she had no control over. So she might as well get used to it and try to embrace Wanda back into her graces, seeing as how she apparently wasn't going anywhere.

Unfortunately though, she couldn't reach Kyle on his cell phone and there was no answer when she called their house. She left a message and started to call her mother when her phone rang in her hand. She answered it quickly, thinking it was Kyle calling her back. "Hello?"

"Hey, girl."

"Oh, hey Charlie. What's going on?"

"Nothing much. I just had a break in the action and thought I'd give you a call. How's your day going?"

"Really well. I did a couple of houses this morning, I talked to my brother Colin, and...Jacob called."

Charlie gasped. "He did? Well it's about time! What'd he say?"

"He asked me out for tonight."

"Whoohoo!" Charlie cheered, making Sahara laugh. "So what time are y'all meeting up?"

"Well, if I don't find someone to watch Rison, never. I can't get in touch with Kyle."

"Oh girl, don't worry about that. I'll watch her."

"Really?" The thought had never even occurred to Sahara, although she had no problem with it whatsoever. Rison had grown to start calling Charlie 'Auntie Charlie' and Sahara totally trusted her with her child. "I'd appreciate that, thanks!"

"Please. It's no problem at all. You know what you're gonna wear yet?"

Sahara started gushing with her friend about guys and clothes, feeling like a teenager. Even when she *was* in high school, she didn't do much of that. It felt kinda good to do it now, even if she did feel a little silly getting all worked up over a guy she had only talked to once and hadn't even met in person yet.

Later on that evening, Charlie came over to stay with Rison and Sahara left out to meet Jacob. She was excited about their date but she was so nervous she was actually shaking a little bit. She didn't know what to expect, but she just hoped that Jacob was nice and that they had a good time together. That's all she allowed herself to wish for. She didn't want to hope for much more than that.

When she got to the restaurant, she asked the hostess if a Jacob Ericson had arrived yet. As the hostess led her to the table, Sahara nervously rubbed her hands together and tried to calm herself down. She didn't want to appear like this was her first date or that she had never been out with a man. She briefly closed her eyes and prayed that Jacob looked as good as the picture she saw and that he was as nice as he seemed to be. Something in her *really* needed this date to go well.

When she arrived at the table, a very handsome gentleman stood up and smiled. She recognized him from the picture and was pleasantly surprised that he looked even better than she expected.

"Thank you, Jesus," she whispered to herself.

"Sahara," Jacob said as the hostess walked off, holding his hand out to her, "It's so good to finally meet you. I'm Jacob."

Sahara placed her hand in his and felt her body immediately warm up. "Hi, Jacob. I'm glad to finally meet you, too." She smiled nervously.

Jacob held her chair out for her and she eased down into it, getting a whiff of what smelled like Polo cologne. It only made her more attracted to him.

"You're pretty nervous, huh?" he asked after he had reclaimed his seat.

Sahara looked at him, surprised. She relaxed a little when she saw he wasn't making fun of her. "Is it that obvious?"

"A little," he said, chuckling. "Don't worry about it, though. I'm a little nervous myself. Auntie talked you up so much to me that I almost didn't even feel worthy of asking you out."

"Really?" Sahara asked, immediately curious about what Ms. Ericson could have said.

"Most definitely. She just went on and on about how sweet and how good a person you are, not to mention your beauty and humility."

"Oh gosh," Sahara said, blushing. She always appreciated a compliment.

"I have to say, though, that Auntie underestimated how beautiful you are. I hope you don't think that's some kind of line, but you really are gorgeous."

Sahara's face was on fire. She knew she wasn't bad-looking, but she never really gave much thought to her looks. People had often told her she was beautiful or whatever and while she always appreciated it, she just took it with a grain of salt. It just didn't feel right to her to gloat about something that she had nothing to do with.

"Thank you, Jacob," she said, her hand on her chest. She forced her eyes to look into his.

"Just giving credit where it's due."

Sahara wanted to tell him how good he looked, but she didn't have the nerve to do it.

"So what looks good to you?" Sahara asked, opening her menu and trying not to drop it since her hands were still slightly shaking.

"I could give the obvious answer and say you, but since I've already fawned over your looks, I'll say the shrimp scampi and the lobster tail," Jacob answered.

"Oh," Sahara said, still blushing. She wondered if she would ever get used to all the compliments if he chose to dole them out on a regular basis. Her eyes scanned the menu as she tried to will herself to relax. "The mahi mahi looks really good to me. I think I'm gonna have that."

"Let's make it happen then," he said, waving the waitress over. He gave her their orders and when she had walked off, he folded his arms on the table, looking at Sahara intently. She tried to appear unfazed. "So how do we get this getting-to-know-you process off the ground? I'm not the best at it."

"Well we might be doomed, then, because I'm probably worse than you."

Jacob chuckled. "Damn, well one of us better get with it, then. 'Cause I *do* want to get to know you."

"And I want to get to know you," Sahara responded shyly. She looked into his handsome face. "So...tell me something about yourself."

They proceeded to take turns talking about themselves through dinner, dessert, and coffee. Sahara was amazed that they got along so well; it was like they had known each other for years. It was almost unbelievable that they were just meeting for the first time that night. By the time she was savoring her carrot cake, she had completely relaxed and found herself dreading the end of the evening. She sincerely was enjoying herself and his company. Jacob was a delight and she couldn't believe no one had snatched him up yet. She would have to give Ms. Ericson a big hug the next time she saw her.

Sahara also found that her body liked Jacob, as well. His looks, the way he smelled, his sense of humor, his charm...all of that combined to melt away all of her nervousness and anxiety and leave nothing but raw attraction and desire. Even though she knew it was way too soon to be even thinking about anything physical, she couldn't deny that it was crossing her mind the more she stayed in his company. She found herself wondering if he was as good a lover as she was imagining him to be. She blushed at the thought.

When the subject of relationships and marriage came up, though, she quieted down a little bit. She wasn't particularly eager to tell him all about her failed marriage. Even though she knew the demise of it wasn't her fault, she didn't want him to think that she wasn't woman enough to keep her man's attention.

"So you want to get married one day?" she asked him.

"Oh, most definitely," he said, pushing aside the plate littered with the crumbs from his cheesecake. "I think marriage is a beautiful thing, but it has to be with the right person. And it takes time to determine that. Too many people just jump into it without any thought. I want to take my time getting to know the woman I'm going to marry and letting her get to know me."

"That sounds good," Sahara said. Even after all the time she was with Kyle, she felt like she didn't really know him. It was too bad it took years for her to realize that, though.

"I look forward to getting married," Jacob continued. "When I do it, though, I want it to be for life. Divorce is not an option for me. That's why I want to take my time and do it right."

Sahara nodded, but couldn't bring herself to respond. She remembered when she had that same outlook about marriage; she had only wanted to get married once and keep that same husband until the day she died. And she had been willing to do that. But here she was, divorced and raising a child alone. Despite all the encouragement from family and friends and the progress she had made since initially learning of Kyle's infidelity, it didn't leave her with the most encouraging opinion of holy matrimony. She was open to dating and maybe even falling in love and being in a monogamous relationship, but she honestly didn't know if she wanted to go down the aisle again.

Sahara was surprised when she looked at her watch and realized three hours had passed. She needed to get home to Rison, but she definitely knew she wanted to see Jacob again. Their date had turned out better than she could ever have expected.

As she and Jacob walked to her car, walking close together but not really touching, his hands in her pockets and hers clasped together, she wondered what would happen next. Would he ask her out again immediately or wait until he called her again? Was she being to presumptuous to think he would ask her out again *at all*? She had certainly had a good time with him but she had no way of being sure if the feeling was mutual.

If it turned out that it wasn't, then it would only prove that she was in fact awful when it came to reading men.

"So Sahara," Jacob began when they reached her indigo blue Altima, "I really, really had a good time with you this evening. You're everything Auntie said you would be."

"I'm glad," Sahara said, heaving an internal sigh of relief. "I had a good time, too."

"I just hate the evening has to end already," he said, looking at her in a way that made her have to squeeze her legs together.

"So do I. But its getting late and I need to get on home to my daughter."

"It's all good. I understand." He took a step closer to her and she took a deep breath, not sure if he was going try to kiss her or if he was just moving closer to her for no reason. "We're seeing each other again, right? I can't just see you once."

Sahara blushed, despite telling herself that she was going to stop doing that so much. "I thought you'd never ask."

Jacob smiled and just gazed into Sahara's eyes. She forced herself to hold the gaze as she tried to control her quivering body. She braced herself against her car, feeling the coldness on her back through her dress. Jacob reached and rested his hand on her car next to her shoulder and Sahara got a good glimpse of his lips, which were moist and beautifully shaped.

"Sahara," he breathed in a low voice, looking at her lips as well, "May I *please* kiss you?"

There was no way she could speak right then, so she simply nodded. He leaned in and gently claimed her lips with his, his large hand taking a slight grasp of her arm. Sahara's eyes slid closed as she acclimated herself to another man's mouth, another man's touch, and after a few seconds, another man's tongue against hers. A tiny moan emitted from her throat as a deeper one resonated from his, both of them savoring and enjoying this first kiss between them.

The kiss lasted for a few minutes, with Sahara resisting the urge to fully wrap her arms around his neck and just settling for resting her hands on his toned biceps. Her body was screaming with desire as thoughts of all the lonely nights in her bed alone came roaring back to her. She couldn't help but think of Jacob between her crisp cotton sheets, and as their kiss deepened, Jacob between her crisp cotton sheets on top of her. She wanted him, plain and simple. But she knew it was too soon to even take it there, regardless of how much she felt she liked him in that moment.

Jacob reluctantly pulled away from Sahara, his hand cupping her chin. He ran his curled fingers up and down her smooth face a few times before kissing her forehead and stepping back. Sahara tried to gather herself, her lips and body already missing and yearning for his.

"I'll give you a call in a little while, okay? Just to make sure you made it home all right," he said, his voice gruff and thick.

Sahara cleared her throat. "Okay," she whispered.

He stepped back so she could get into her car. Sahara placed her long legs inside and Jacob closed the door, his eyes still on her. Sahara just hoped she would be able to remember how to drive as she put her key in the ignition and pulled off.

CHAPTER TEN

The Saturday after Sahara's date with Jacob, she and Rison were sitting at their kitchen table enjoying a breakfast of waffles, bacon, and fruit. Sahara's mind kept wandering to Jacob, as hard as she tried to just focus on her daughter. Rison got her attention for good, though, when she asked, "Mommy, am I gonna get a new daddy?"

Sahara almost choked on her bacon and she took a sip of her apple juice. Rison always asked these kinds of questions when she was least expecting it. "No, sweetie. You're not going to get a new daddy." There was no need to ask why she would ask such a thing, since Kyle still wasn't making any kind of effort to come to see her.

"So I'm not gonna have a daddy?"

"You have one already, sweetie. He's just been busy lately, that's all."

Rison didn't respond. She just picked up a piece of cantaloupe and nibbled around the edge. Sahara didn't know if that meant she was satisfied with her answer or if she was simply thinking of what question to ask next.

Sahara had decided to not even worry about Kyle anymore since he was evidently too busy to make time for Rison. He didn't even call and talk to her that much, let alone come and see her. Sahara had tried to call him on a few occasions but could never get in touch with him, and her messages went unanswered. She could only figure that he was either really busy at work or reveling in his relationship with her cousin, or both.

Nevertheless, she wasn't going to continue to try to reach out to him and get him to come and see his own child that he claimed to love so much. Rison's questions about him were coming slightly less often, and Sahara made sure to never say anything negative about Kyle to her. She just tried to lavish her with as much attention as she could and let her know that her mommy loved her more than anything. It might not be ideal but Sahara hoped that it would do.

The next day at church, Sahara sat with Charlie, feeling more renewed and free than she had in a while. It was the first Sunday since her split with Kyle that she didn't feel weighed down with sadness and anguish, praying for the Lord to bring her through this rough time in her life. She was feeling like her prayers were finally being answered.

The more she thought about it, the more she realized that Kyle simply wasn't the man for her. He couldn't have been, if he could do something like he did. And she didn't even want to get started on the way he was treating Rison. His leaving her was one thing, but she at *least* thought that his relationship with their child would stay in tact. Never in a million years would she have thought that he would continuously stand her up and not even bother to call and see how she's doing. And since he wasn't returning any of Sahara's calls, she could only conclude that he just didn't care. What else could it be? Sahara knew that Rison deserved better than that and so did she.

She had to admit, Kyle had done her a favor by leaving. She didn't need a man like him.

During the course of the service, Sahara noticed Charlie occasionally looking somewhere over her shoulder towards the back of the sanctuary. Sahara itched to turn and see what it was she kept looking at, but she resisted. When the service was over, Charlie eagerly waved someone over them. Sahara cringed when she saw a tall man with deep dimples and dark caramel skin come heading their way. She looked at Charlie with slightly narrowed eyes as she slid a polite smile onto her face, wondering what her friend was up to. Charlie just grinned at her.

"I'm glad you could make it," Charlie said to her good-looking friend, reaching up to hug him.

"Thank you for inviting me," the man said, his voice surprising Sahara. She had never heard a voice so deep in person. "I'm sorry I didn't make it here on time. I guess I was moving too slow this morning."

"Don't worry about it. You're here; that's what's important." She turned eagerly to Sahara, who was standing there patiently, wondering who this man was. She didn't know if he was someone Charlie was dating or a relative or what.

"Sahara," Charlie began, "this is Shannon Ephram. He's a friend of mine from work. Shannon, this is Sahara Johnson, the one I was telling you about."

Sahara looked at Charlie curiously but stuck her hand out to Shannon, still smiling. "Hi, Shannon. It's nice to meet you."

"You too, Sahara. Charlie here had told me a lot about you over the past couple of weeks. I feel like I know you already."

"Really? Well, I wish I could say the same," she replied, looking at Charlie pointedly.

Charlie leaned in close to Sahara and said in a low voice, "I told you I was going to introduce you to some men, girl. Did you think I was joking?"

"No, I just didn't expect it *today*," Sahara hissed back.

"How long was I supposed to wait? There's no time like the present." Charlie looked at Shannon, who Sahara had to admit was quite a looker. He towered over her and was very dashing in the light tan suit he was wearing. He had a ruggedness about him that Sahara found herself immediately drawn to, but he still carried himself in a poised, confident manner. Like he would be comfortable in a boardroom or on the block.

"Did you enjoy the service?" Sahara asked him.

"Oh yes, very much," Shannon responded. "Pastor Roy reminds me of the preacher I grew up with back home. He wasn't all about entertaining like so many preachers nowadays; just teaching the Word. That's what it's all about."

Sahara liked this man. She had only known him for two minutes, but she liked him.

"I couldn't agree with you more," she replied, smiling. "I have yet to hear one of his sermons that I didn't get something out of. He's amazing."

"Yes, he is."

"You know what? I think I see somebody I know *way* over there. Will y'all excuse me?" Charlie said hastily, pretending to wave to somebody across the sanctuary and head off in that direction. Sahara wanted to reach out and grab her arm but she stopped herself, not wanting to give Shannon the impression that she didn't want to talk to him.

"Real subtle, huh?" Shannon said, chuckling.

"Yeah, I know, right," Sahara laughed. "I think she really wants us to hit it off."

"I don't think that'll be too hard," Shannon replied, smiling at her. "We seem to be hitting it off okay."

"Yeah."

"Of course, it might gain us more headway in that direction if you, say, gave me your number."

This man sure doesn't waste any time, Sahara thought. Regardless, though, she found herself reaching into her purse and pulling out one of her business cards. She handed it to him and watched as she held it in his huge hand, his dark eyes roaming her elegant raised lettering. "A cleaning business, huh? I know some people who would be interested in your services, like yesterday. Do you have any more on you so I can give them out?"

"Of course," Sahara said, pulling out a few more cards. She was liking him more and more. "I appreciate any referrals. If you send a few people to me, I might have to come and clean a couple of rooms for you in *your* house." She was partially kidding, but liked the idea her flippant comment had inspired. She needed to have a referral program for her business. She made a mental note to do something about that.

"Girl, you just made a friend just then," Shannon joked, prompting a giggle from Sahara. "But I wouldn't want you doing any more of that than necessary. I keep my place pretty clean. And while I think it's awesome that you have your own thing going on, I just can't imagine you on your knees scrubbing floors and cleaning ovens."

"What could you imagine me doing?" Sahara asked, hoping the question wouldn't be considered suggestive.

"I don't know, really. Maybe running things while your employees did the dirty work."

"Oh, well I don't mind the work. I actually enjoy it. Maybe one day I'll get to where I have a staff and I don't have to do the actual cleaning anymore, just heading things up from the office."

"You can do that. It seems like you're well on your way. I admire anyone who has the courage to step out on their own."

Sahara flashed him a proud smile. The truth of the matter was, she was proud of herself for growing and maintaining her business, especially in the midst of everything that had been going on in her life. She was able to support her child and herself without having to answer to anybody else. And it would only get better.

She found herself feeling really comfortable around Shannon. There wasn't any of the nervousness that consumed her before her date with Jacob. Perhaps that was because there wasn't any of the anticipation that she had on her date. Meeting Shannon had been totally unexpected.

Speaking of Jacob, they had talked every night since their date a few nights ago. The more they talked, the more she was attracted to him. A second date was definitely happening. She was really looking forward to it and to be honest, hoping to get another one of those incredible kisses from him. That kiss had been stuck in her mind since that night. She couldn't forget about that no more than she had been able to get her body to stop yearning for his hands to be on it. It had been a while since she had wanted a man so much.

But this Shannon seemed like a really nice guy, too, and she knew Charlie wouldn't have introduced her to him if he wasn't. Sahara noticed Charlie standing a little ways off, not doing a very good job of pretending to not be trying to hear their every word. She just shook her head and chuckled to herself.

As she continued to talk to Shannon and the occasional church member that came over to give her a hug or shake her hand, Kyle watched her from the far opposite side of the sanctuary. He hadn't seen or talked to her since the night he went by her place and saw her with that woman. He hadn't said anything to Wanda about it, mostly because he still couldn't believe it himself. There was no way he would have imagined that he would be able to devastate a woman so much that she would give up on men altogether and start rubbing up against her own gender.

He stood there watching as she talked to that man (who he couldn't help wondering where he came from and who he was to Sahara), and sneaking looks over to her lover, who stood a few feet away. It ate him up that his daughter was being raised in a lesbian household, and he knew that he would have to get on the ball when it came to getting custody of her. Although he knew that in not taking any of Sahara's calls or going over there because he didn't want to see her, he also wasn't seeing Rison and that by no means was a good thing, he just couldn't get the image of Sahara and that woman out of his head. To him, Sahara was being irresponsible and reckless and that was unforgivable to him.

Wanda came over to him, looking to see what he was staring at so intently. She wasn't happy to see it was his ex-wife. "Why are you looking at her like that?" she asked, with slight attitude in her voice.

Kyle hesitated only a second before he answered. "I found out something very disturbing out Sahara."

"What?"

"That she's gone over to the other side."

Wanda frowned. "The other side of what, Kyle?"

"She's gay, Wanda."

"What do you mean, she's gay?"

"I certainly don't mean gay as in happy."

"You trying to tell me she's a lesbian?"

"Yep."

Wanda looked over at Sahara, who was talking to some man she had never seen before. He must have been a visitor or a new member, although she couldn't very well say that she kept up with the regular members of the church. She really only went out of habit and because Kyle wanted her to. She didn't know who the man was that Sahara was talking to but she had to admit he was fine as hell. Her cousin certainly had good taste; if she hadn't already stolen Kyle from her she might have to steal this one too.

But from the looks of it, Sahara looked to be making eyes at that tall hunk and not paying attention to any woman. Kyle had to be mistaken. Wanda crossed her arms. "And just how do you know that, Kyle?"

"Let's just say I saw more than I wanted to see. Trust me, I know what I'm talking about here."

Wanda peered at her tame cousin and just shook her head. She couldn't believe Sahara would go that route and was a little disgusted at the thought of two women together (although she had participated in her share of threesomes over the years), she had to admit she was a little impressed that Sahara would do something like that. Wanda never thought she would have it in her.

Meanwhile, Sahara and Shannon had claimed a seat on one of the pews and were deep in conversation when Charlie walked back over to them. She had to clear her throat loudly just to get their attention.

"Ah, I hate to break this up, but I'm getting hungry," she announced.

"What do you say I take you ladies to brunch? I know this restaurant that makes Belgian waffles that just melt in your mouth."

"Sounds good to me," Charlie said. "Sahara?"

"My stomach is already growling. I'll just have to go get Rison from the nursery and then we can leave."

"Cool. I'm gonna go get the car and I'll meet you out in the parking lot."

"All right," Charlie said, claiming Shannon's seat when he got up to head outside. Once he was out of earshot, she leaned into a grinning Sahara. "I guess I don't have to ask what you think, huh? You two forgot all about little ol' me."

"I wouldn't say all that. But I have to admit; I *do* like him."

"I knew you would. Just give me half of your waffle at brunch and we'll call it even."

Sahara laughed as she stood up. "Yeah, right. You're gonna have to think of something else. And let's not jump the gun here; Shannon and I just met. Its not like we're headed down the aisle or anything."

"Could happen, one day," Charlie said, standing up herself. "I know for a fact that Shannon wants to get married at some point. And he's a really good man and y'all look so good together. I could see it happening."

"Girl, I am so far off from marrying *anybody*, regardless of who it is. But we'll see how it goes."

"Yes, we will," Charlie said, grabbing her purse. "Now let's go get Rison so we can eat. I'm starving like a mug. We don't want to keep your future boo waiting."

CHAPTER ELEVEN

Well, it seemed official; Sahara was seeing two men at once.

It was a first that she couldn't believe was happening. There was a very small part of her that felt a little bad about it, but she figured that as long as she was honest with them both, she wasn't really doing anything wrong. She wasn't married anymore or committed to anybody; there was no law that said she only had to date one man at a time.

Sahara was honest with both Jacob and Shannon that she wasn't ready for a heavy relationship or to be totally exclusive with anybody. As much she liked them both, she needed to keep things casual. All she really wanted to do for the time being was have some fun. They both seemed to understand that, given what she had been through. She was glad because she honestly didn't know which one of them she liked the most and wasn't ready to stop seeing either of them.

She practically gushed when she told her mother about her two suitors.

"Mama, I've never been in a position like this," she said over the phone one night. She was absentmindedly watching a movie while Rison slept in her room. "Two incredible men actually want me and I kind of want both of them back!"

Julia chuckled. "I guess there's nothing like being wanted. And there's no reason any man in his right mind wouldn't want you."

"Aww, thank you, Mama," Sahara said appreciatively. "They're both so smooth and have an alluring aura about them, but Jacob's is more in-your-face while Shannon's is more subtle. I don't know which one attracts me the most."

"You don't have to decide just yet. Just enjoy it. You deserve to have a good time. I just want to caution you, though, to be careful about what you do in front of Rison. While you have the right to date whoever you want, remember you have a daughter watching you. She doesn't need to see her mother with a parade of men coming in and out."

"Come on, Mama. You know I wouldn't have them up in here like that."

"I'm sure you wouldn't, baby. Don't take it personally. I just know how it is when you're in the beginning stages of a new relationship; you get so caught up in the thrill of it that you might not make the best choices. And especially in your case, since you're so new to all this because all you know is Kyle. I'm just saying to be mindful of it. That's all."

"You're right," Sahara admitted, calming down. She had actually started to take offense to what her mother was saying, thinking that her mother should know she would have more sense than that but when she thought about it, it was only right. She *did* need to watch what she did in front of Rison. Lord knows that little girl had enough to deal with as it was. It was gonna be difficult enough explaining that she was even going to be *dating* other men besides her father, let alone more than one. But she would cross that bridge when she got to it.

As it stood, it was still too early to even consider letting Shannon or Jacob around her daughter like that. Sure, Shannon had been there when they all went out to brunch on the day they met, but for all Rison knew, Shannon was with Charlie or just some man they were eating with. It's not like Sahara had been all hugged up with him. Shannon and Rison had gotten along well, though, so that was good.

Sahara really appreciated her mother for encouraging her and telling her the truth. And over the next few weeks, Julia had begun keeping Rison more because Sahara's had become busier with work. Sahara had to think that was in part thanks to Shannon's referrals. Things had started to pick up not too long after they met. It was just one more reason to like him.

Among her new clients was a very handsome man named Tony. He worked from home a lot and was usually holed up in his office while Sahara cleaned, but he would always come out when she was done and talk to her for a little while. One day out of the blue, he asked her out. While flattered, Sahara had to decline because she didn't really want to start dating her clients. It would just be too complicated.

But she couldn't deny that she was incredibly attracted to Tony. He was bow-legged, which Sahara had always loved on a man, with a neatly trimmed beard and some of the most beautiful dreadlocs she had ever seen. They were jet black and hung past his shoulders. Sahara found herself wanting to run her hands through them just to see how they felt.

She didn't know what was happening to her, being physically attracted to so many men at once. This was a definite first. Maybe before, she had been so focused on Kyle that she just didn't notice other men, but she certainly was now. She lusted after Jacob after just one date, a bear hug from Shannon had her panties wet, and now the scent of whatever oil it was Tony was wearing was causing her nipples to harden and making her want to lick her lips with a slow tongue.

Gosh, what had *happened* to her?

She was a healthy, heterosexual woman; it was only natural that her body would respond to attractive men. She couldn't imagine that there was anything *really* wrong with that. But this was all just so new to her; now there were *three* men roaming through her imaginary bedroom. Sahara could just imagine what scenarios would be coursing through her mind about Tony in addition to the ones already saturating it involving Jacob and Shannon. It just all seemed so...*wicked*. She couldn't help feeling a little guilty.

That night after she had gotten Rison into bed and taken a shower, she dropped to her knees and clasped her hands together tightly, praying for forgiveness for thinking sexual thoughts about three different men.

CHAPTER TWELVE

Sahara and Charlie were at the gym one Saturday, running alongside each other on the treadmills.

"How was your date with Shannon last night?" Charlie asked, panting slightly.

"It was great, as usual," Sahara responded, wiping her sweaty face with a towel before tucking it back into the waistband of her blue track pants. "He arranged a private dinner at the beach, and afterwards we walked up and down the shore, talking about any and everything. It was the most beautiful date I've been on. I loved it."

"I told you...Shannon was something," Charlie replied, trying to keep her breath. She glanced over at Sahara, who was running effortlessly at a speed of six miles per hour. Charlie was jogging at almost five and was starting to feel it.

"He is," Sahara confirmed.

"What about...Jacob? When are you...seeing him...again?"

"Tonight. I'm really looking forward to it."

"Where's...he taking you? Do...do you know?"

"Nope, he hasn't told me. He just told me to dress comfortably."

"Dress...comfortably, huh? Well, he...certainly has...my interest piqued."

"Mine, too. About a lot of things."

Charlie glanced over at Sahara. "What...does that mean?"

Sahara started to blush, peeking at Charlie. "It's a little embarrassing..."

"Hold up, girl...let's slow down so I can...give you my full attention," Charlie panted, decreasing the speed on the treadmill to a brisk walk. She was grateful for the excuse to slow down because her thighs were burning something terrible.

Sahara slowed down to a slow trot. She wasn't as winded as Charlie; plus, she had a *lot* of repressed sexual energy to burn off. "To be honest with you, Charlie, I've been having a lot of very...lustful thoughts about both Jacob and Shannon..."

"There's nothing wrong with that, girl."

"...and Tony."

Charlie smirked, noticing Sahara's embarrassment at admitting that she lusted after three different men. She had no doubt that this was unchartered territory for her friend. "Remind me who Tony is again?"

"He's the client of mine who works from home and has those amazing dreads."

"Oh, yeah."

"He's asked me out a couple of times and I always turn him down, but I can't help but be *so* attracted to him. He's just so exotic and earthy and rough-around-the-edges. I can't seem to get him out of my mind."

"So what's the problem?"

"It just seems wrong to me to be thinking these kinds of thoughts about three different men at once."

"Wrong to whom?"

"Well...to me, I guess."

"I mean, really, what's wrong with it? Its not like you're actually acting out whatever it is you're thinking about." She quickly glanced over at Sahara. "*Are* you?"

"Of course not!" Sahara quickly replied. "I haven't gone there with *any* of them. I haven't done that with anybody since Kyle. But I really, really can't say that I don't want to."

"It's only natural, Sahara. You have three sexy men after you."

"Well yeah, but-"

"Quit worrying so much about what you think you *should* be thinking and just enjoy *thinking* it. And if it goes there, it goes there. You're a grown woman who has a new lease on life. Just enjoy it."

"But, but I have a child!"

Charlie laughed. It was amazing how innocent Sahara really was. "I understand that, but where does it say that you can't have a child and have fun, too? Sahara, for real. You're a good mother, you're responsible, and you handle your business. As long as you don't let anything interfere with that, you shouldn't have a problem. Just do what's in your heart and stop thinking so much. Don't be so inhibited."

Sahara really didn't know how to be any other way.

During the rest of their workout, she thought about her and Charlie's conversation. She would love to just throw all caution to the wind and do whatever she wanted. But Rison was always in the back of her mind. She didn't want to become irresponsible or start acting anything the way Kyle was acting. Rison had to come first.

But being carefree *did* have a certain intrigue. And if she didn't do it now, when would she ever do it? She wouldn't be young and desirable forever. If she was going to have an active social life, the time was now.

She began to look forward to going over to Tony's. He had hired her on a twice-a-week basis and she couldn't help but think that it was because he just wanted to see more of her, because since he lived alone and spent a lot of time in his office, during her second visit of the week there really wasn't a whole lot to do. He didn't spend most of the time in his office like he usually did when she was there working; he spent a lot of it trying to talk to her and get to know her, and over time Sahara opened up to him more and more. And he still flirted endlessly, which she didn't mind; in fact, she even allowed herself to flirt back a little bit.

But she still didn't want to date him, though. If he wasn't one of her clients, she would have. But business had to come before pleasure, and she couldn't drop him as a client just to be able to go out with him. What if it didn't work out? She had her hands full with Jacob and Shannon, anyway.

One particular day had been very busy. She had gone out with Jacob the night before and then had to be up at six the next morning in order to get started on a five-house day. Tony's was her next to last one and she was more than a little tired. She was grateful that she wouldn't have to do a whole lot of actual cleaning, since he kept things up pretty well in between her visits.

"You're quite tired today, huh?" Tony asked as she swept his small kitchen.

Sahara looked up and gave a small smile. "Is it that obvious?"

"A little bit."

"I guess I look pretty bad, huh?"

"Not at all," Tony said, his voice carrying slight traces of his Caribbean heritage. "Even when you're tired you are exquisite."

Sahara blushed. "Aww...thanks Tony." She felt her body waking up, with him standing there watching her like that.

He leaned his head against the door frame, his hands in the pockets of his cargo shorts. "I see you're almost done. Can I get you anything to drink?"

"No, thank you. I'm fine."

"Most definitely," Tony said, eyeing her seductively under his long lashes.

Sahara blushed as she willed her hands to stop quivering. She gripped the broom she held in her hands tighter. "Um, did you want to go and check my work? I'll be done in a minute and I have another job after this."

"Oh, I'm sure everything is just as it should be," Tony said with a wave of his hand, moving towards her. "You always do exceptional work. Why don't you rest for a minute before you leave?" he asked, reaching in and slowly removing the broom from her slightly shaking hands. "Take a load off."

Sahara's feet wanted her to take him up on that offer, but her head knew that if she did she might not even make it to her next appointment. "As tempting as that sounds, I need to go ahead and wrap things up here so I can make it to my next house on time." She turned and busied herself with gathering her cleaning supplies. He was standing rather close to her now and it was becoming harder and harder for her to keep her composure. She wanted to just bury her hands in all those gorgeous dreads and kiss him silly.

"So when will I get to see you again?" he asked.

"Ahh, I come back on Monday. Or did you need to change the day?"

"Why don't you just come by and see me instead of worrying about cleaning anything? We can just hang out, watch a movie or something."

Sahara smiled. Everything in her wanted to accept his offer, but she knew it wouldn't be the sensible thing to do. That would be too much like a date. "I can't do that, Tony."

"No? How come? Oh, you're worried about losing out on the business, huh? Tell you what, I'll still pay you for your time. How does that sound?"

Sahara chuckled. "That's not necessary."

"So you'll come for free?"

"I can't."

He stepped up really close behind her and she immediately held her breath, anticipating his possible touch. She wanted him to reach for her but she knew she would have to go through the charade of acting like she didn't want him to. It was better if he just kept his hands to himself, even if her body was aching for him to do just the opposite.

"You can't because you don't want to or you can't because you don't want to be unprofessional?"

"Its one of those," Sahara said in a low voice, her back still to him.

"Can I guess which one?" he asked, gently grabbing her arm and turning her around to face him.

Oh, how Sahara loved the way he smelled. The deep, earthy body oil that he wore made her just want to lean in and inhale every inch of his skin. And the way he was gazing at her underneath those beautiful long lashes was causing her knees to get weaker and weaker by the second.

"Sahara..." he breathed, licking his lips.

"Tony...I really have to go," she said quickly, her voice a mere whisper. She gingerly placed her hands against his chest to stop him from inching any closer to her, all the while forcing herself to not look at those beautiful lips that he insisted on licking seductively right in front of her.

Tony just held her arms for a moment, his eyes taking in all of her face. He looked like he wanted to kiss her and part of Sahara wanted to let him, even if it wasn't the wisest thing to let happen. She prepared herself for his approach, still unsure of whether she would receive him or reject him, when he let go of her arms and stepped back. Sahara realized just how fast her heart had been beating.

"Until next time, huh?"

Sahara didn't quite know how to respond to that, so she just gave a small nod and went about getting her things together.

Once she was out inside her car, she took a minute to get herself together. She recalled how close Tony had been standing to her and touched her arms where his hands had gripped them. Part of her was somewhat disappointed that he didn't in fact try to kiss her; even after all the lectures she had been giving herself to keep things professional between them, she knew she most likely would have done nothing more than lean in and wrap her arms around his neck, matching whatever level of intensity he laid out.

She headed off to her next appointment. Her cell phone rang in her pocket and she got it out right before it went to voice mail. It was her client, saying she needed to go out for the evening and would have to cancel her appointment. Sahara was relieved, glad to get to go home early. She called Julia to let her know she was on her way to get Rison.

While she was on with her mother, she got a call from Shannon, inviting her out to dinner. Even though she was incredibly tired, she perked up at the thought of spending an evening with Shannon. She missed him, after not seeing him for a few days. So she accepted his invitation and agreed to meet him in the next hour, and then clicked over and told her mother that she would be a little late getting Rison, not thinking it necessary to tell her that it was for a date and not because she was working.

Might as well start trying this carefree thing now, she thought with an eager smile.

CHAPTER THIRTEEN

Across town, Kyle sat in his home office, tapping a pen against the desk. Try as he might, he couldn't get his mind off his ex-wife.

There was no way in the world that he would ever have pegged Sahara for becoming a lesbian. Did his leaving her crush her so much that she was turned off of men altogether? He had expected her to be hurt but he didn't think she would abandon the entire male population. While part of him was disturbed by it, part of him couldn't help being a little flattered that he would be the last man she deemed worthy of being with.

He really felt responsible for turning Sahara against men. It was on his mind constantly since that night he saw her with that woman at her apartment and again at church. Part of him wondered who that man was that she was talking to after the service but it never entered his mind that it was someone that she could be seeing. All he had been focused on was Sahara and the woman standing a few feet away watching her. To him, they were making serious eyes at each other. How long had this been going on? Since the night he had rejected her? Did it devastate her so much that it drove her into the comforting arms of one of her girlfriends, and what started out as platonic, sisterly consoling evolved into a passionate, eye-opening session on explorative lovemaking?

And where was Rison when all of this was going on? He was upset about his daughter possibly seeing or hearing something that she wasn't ready for or wouldn't understand, but he tried to cut Sahara a little slack. She had been through a lot over the past year. Maybe he should try to talk to her; see where her head was at. Maybe they could come to some sort of understanding.

He called her on her cell phone, but it rolled over to voice mail. He tried again, thinking maybe she just didn't have time to get to the phone the first time. She didn't answer until the third call, and she did *not* sound very happy to hear from him.

"What?" she asked in an angry whisper.

"Are you busy?"

"You didn't gather that from my not answering the phone the first two times you called? What do you want?"

"I need to talk to you. It's kind of important."

"Well, it's going to have to wait. I'm on a date."

"*Another* date? I mean…good for you. Um, so you're out with Charlie again, huh? Y'all really seem to be hitting it off."

"Yes, we did. But I'm not out with Charlie."

He automatically started to ask who she was out with, but held his tongue. Even though he really, really wanted to know. "Oh…"

It sounded like she had put her hand over the phone while he heard her saying something to her date. He strained to hear what she was saying but he couldn't really make anything out. At the end of it, he heard her say, "Just one second, Shannon," before she got back to Kyle. "I have to go."

Shannon?? Kyle was floored. She was out with yet *another* woman? What happened to Charlie? Maybe *he* was the guy that made her turn over to women. Just how many people was she dating? And where the heck was Rison??

"May I ask where my child is?" he asked, not being able to keep the sarcasm out of his voice.

"You don't need to worry about that," Sahara hissed angrily. "I've taken care of that just like I've been doing for the past few months while you're off living like a childless bachelor. Now goodbye." She hung up.

Kyle wanted to throw the phone across the room. Now not only was Sahara dating women, she was apparently seeing more than one. And all around his daughter. This was just completely and totally unacceptable.

He got up and stalked down to the kitchen, where Wanda was heating up some soup on the stove. That was about the extent of her cooking skills. Anything out of a can or a package or a bag, but nothing from scratch. Kyle sometimes missed a good old-fashioned, home cooked meal like the ones Sahara used to make for him every night, but he just chose to overlook that minor little flaw in his bride-to-be.

"Hey, baby," he said, easing up on one of the stools that surrounded the kitchen island.

"Hey," Wanda responded, stirring her tomato soup. She glanced back at him. "You look like you have something on your mind. What's up?"

"I just got off the phone with Sahara," he said.

"Oh?" Wanda tried not to show the attitude that automatically flared up in her. She was getting a little tired of hearing about Sahara. "Did y'all argue or something?"

"Not exactly. She was actually on a date with yet another woman. I couldn't believe it."

Wanda put her spoon down and turned to look at Kyle, leaning against the counter. "Did she tell you that?"

"Did she tell me what?"

"That she was out with a woman."

"Not directly, but I'm not an idiot. She called whoever she was with 'Shannon.' What does that tell you?"

"Don't you think that you're jumping to conclusions here, Kyle?"

"Not at all, Wanda. Let's just face it: I've driven my ex-wife to women. Other than some dude named Charlie that she went out with, she's been messing around with women for weeks, apparently. Now the question is, what do we do about it?"

Wanda just shook her head and turned to get a bowl out of the cupboard behind her. She thought Kyle was being a little ridiculous, not to mention arrogant. Personally, she didn't think that her cousin was a lesbian. Nothing Kyle said really proved that. And he was pretty full of himself to think that he had it like that where a woman would just not even try any more men after him. He was handsome and he made good money, but he wasn't all *that*.

And even if Sahara was, in fact, snuggling up with women, it really wasn't any of his business. It annoyed Wanda that Kyle was so absorbed in Sahara's personal life. Why was he so concerned about who she dated? It seemed to run a little deeper than general concern for her well-being or even being worried about Rison, like he always claimed. He actually seemed upset that she was dating other people. What did he think, that she was going to become a nun after he left her?

Wanda just knew one thing: she could care less who her cousin was kissing on and she would have to do a little extra work to make sure Kyle quit worrying about it, too.

"What do you expect us to do about it, Kyle? It's not any of our business who that woman dates, man or woman."

"If she didn't have my child living with her, I would agree with you. But since she does, it is every *bit* my business. I do *not* want my daughter growing up in a lesbian household. What if Sahara moves one of these women in with her and Rison comes up to me telling me she has two mommies or something like that? Do you know how embarrassing that would be?"

"You're tripping."

"Am I? I guess you couldn't understand, since you don't have any kids of your own yet."

And I never will, Wanda thought to herself. She ladled out some of the warmed soup into the bowl.

"I think I need to go ahead and push for custody of Rison," Kyle announced.

Wanda almost dropped her spoon. She whirled around to look at him and noticed the stern, determined look on his face. "Excuse me?"

"You heard what I said. I have to nip this thing in the bud and get my baby girl out of there as soon as I can." He looked up at Wanda. "You're behind me on this, right?"

Wanda swallowed and tried to put on a compassionate face. "You know I got your back on whatever, baby. But let's think about this for a minute." She took a seat on the stool opposite him and took his hands in hers. "Sahara is a good mother. You know it and I know it, right?"

"Yeah..."

"She loves that little girl to death. You know full well she wouldn't do anything to hurt her. I doubt very seriously Sahara would expose Rison to anything inappropriate."

Kyle hadn't really thought of it like that. Sahara had never been reckless or irresponsible, especially where their daughter was concerned. He had no real reason to believe she would start now. "I guess you're right, but..."

"But what, Kyle? Let's get to the real, here. Now I don't mean to sound harsh or anything, but with everything that you've put both of them through in the past year and especially recently, do you really want to add to it by ripping them apart from each other just because you don't like who Sahara chooses to date?"

Kyle sat back a bit, stung a little but at his fiancé's words. "Damn, it's like that, Wanda?"

"I'm just being honest with you. When was the last time you've even *seen* Rison?"

Kyle's mouth hung open, unable to defend himself.

"That's what I thought. You don't even see her at church, when she's down in the nursery. What stops you from doing that?"

That thought had never even occurred to Kyle, and it really embarrassed him. He looked down at the counter in shame.

"From what I gathered from Sahara the last time I talked to her, Rison has been crying for you and was devastated that you hadn't been going over to see her," Wanda continued, laying it on thick. "And now all of a sudden you're going to uproot her from the *one* parent who has been there for her consistently from the beginning? And let's not even get started on what it would do to Sahara to have her daughter taken from her. Its bad enough you left her for me, her own cousin. Haven't you hurt that woman enough?"

Kyle glared at Wanda. She was really trying to make him feel guilty, and he couldn't say that it wasn't working. He knew full well how much he had hurt Sahara, and he knew he hadn't been doing what he should when it came to Rison. At first it was out of selfishness, wanting to spend all his free time with Wanda. Then it was out of stubbornness, not wanting to deal with Sahara after seeing her with that woman in her driveway. He knew it was wrong, but he hadn't been thinking about anything other than himself. And Rison was suffering because of it. There was a very good chance that even if he got the custody of his daughter, she wouldn't even *want* to live with him.

He also noticed that Wanda wasn't mentioning her part in any of this. She was the one that he had cheated on Sahara with and left her for. Sahara was hurt by Wanda's part just like she was by Kyle's. Sure, he was the one she was married to, but Wanda was her cousin. They were *both* in the wrong. But he figured he really wasn't in any kind of position to point fingers.

"All right," he conceded after a couple of minutes. He blew out a frustrated breath. "I'll back off of the custody issue. You satisfied?" He got up and sulked back upstairs.

Wanda let out a relieved sigh. *That was a close one*, she thought to herself. She simply could not let Kyle go through with this whole custody nonsense. There was no way she wanted to live in the same house with a four-year-old. Dealing with her wetting the bed and having to baby sit and wipe snotty noses and watch all those annoying cartoons was not anything she was looking forward to in the slightest. Kyle would just have to be satisfied with going to Sahara's to see his daughter. She might even concede to letting the little brat come over every now and then. But having her live with them? There was no way in hell. Wanda wanted it to just be her and Kyle, and that's all there was to it.

Upstairs, Kyle was mindlessly returning some emails on his computer, his mind still on his conversation with Wanda. He could agree with some of the things she said and the overall message, but that didn't stop him from wanting to have Rison in the house with him twenty-four-seven. And after the wedding, that's exactly what was going to happen, whether Wanda liked it or not.

CHAPTER FOURTEEN

"**D**inner was wonderful, Jacob, thank you so much," Sahara gushed, wiping her mouth delicately with a napkin.

"Glad you enjoyed it," Jacob said, taking her empty plate along with his into the kitchen.

"I had no idea you could cook so well," she called out, brushing some crumbs from her skirt. She stood up a grabbed her wineglass, sipping on the sweet red wine as she sauntered into the kitchen behind Jacob. He was at the sink, rinsing off the dishes.

"Oh, well ya know. I do what I do," he joked, looking over his shoulder at her and giving her a wink.

Sahara's face flushed. She found herself slowly running her finger around the rim of her wineglass and running her eyes appreciatively up and down Jacob's tight, muscular frame. She bit her lip. Ever since she had arrived at Jacob's townhouse, she'd been trying to keep her thoughts from going too far into the forbidden. But it was getting to where she simply wasn't able to help it. The more time she spent with Jacob, the more she was attracted to him, on all levels, but especially physically. Her body was beginning to crave this man something terrible.

After Jacob finished with the dishes (which he refused to let Sahara help with), he took her hand and led her to the patio. He took her glass from her and sat down on the cushioned chaise, pulling her down to sit on his lap. Sahara was glad she was sitting with her back to him because she was taking a bunch of tiny breaths, trying to keep her composure. He had his arms wrapped around her and was pointing out certain stars to her, occasionally kissing her on her neck and lazily stroking her hand. Sahara's behind was right on his crotch and she could feel it stirring underneath her every now and then and she had to resist the natural urge to grind down onto it to wake it up all the way.

"I'm glad you're here," he whispered into her ear, his grip on her tightening slightly. Sahara could feel his breath against her neck.

"Me too," she whispered back.

He was quiet for a moment before he said, "It's a beautiful night tonight."

"Sure is."

"I could get used to this. Being here with you like this."

Sahara didn't really know what to say to that. She just let out a relaxed and lazy moan. She felt him stir underneath her.

"Sahara…" he breathed, his strong hand coming up to caress her face.

She turned towards him slightly, not trusting herself to say anything more than a barely audibly whispered "Yes?" He stared intensely into her eyes and then at her anxious lips as he slowly brought her face to his, sinking his lips onto hers. Their eyes closed simultaneously as they each opened their mouths to each other, not wasting any time with teasing nips or soft pecks. They kissed hungrily, like it was something they had each been waiting for all evening and was *finally* being graced with. It was the long-anticipated dessert to the meal they shared together earlier and they both were looking for generous helpings.

Sahara gripped his shirt as she moaned from the back of her throat, savoring the faint taste of wine on Jacob's tongue and the feel of his fingers on her skin underneath her shirt. Her body was screaming for him to be inside of it and she turned in his lap, ready and willing to throw away any inhibitions or cautious thoughts she may have had, and lifted up her tight pencil skirt so she could straddle him. His hands automatically came and gripped her firm and juicy behind, grunting in pleasure at this first truly intimate feel of her.

"I want you," he breathed against her face, holding it in his unyielding hand as he ran his tongue around the edge of her succulently-shaped lips. "I want you so much, baby..."

Sahara didn't respond with words. She just started lifting his shirt over his head. In the next minute, all of their clothes were strewn across the patio deck. Jacob's head was between Sahara's legs, giving her the first oral pleasure she had received in years. She writhed on the cool cushioned chaise, matching the rhythm of her hips with that of Jacob's tongue, which was stroking her with a mastery that Sahara wondered where he had time to acquire. It was absolutely amazing.

After giving each of Sahara's lush breasts generous and equal attention that had her calling out his name and not caring who heard her, Jacob slipped on a condom and slowly entered into her, sensing that she probably hadn't done this in a while. He made love to her slowly, not wanting to hurt her but wanting to make sure she never forgot him.

After her body adjusted to his size, she wrapped her long legs around him and tried to dance to the rhythm his body was playing to her. It never crossed her mind to be concerned about anybody possibly seeing or hearing them making love outside like they were; she was past worrying about anybody that wasn't named Jacob Ericson right then. He was giving her quite possibly the most erotic night of her life. She had never made love outside and she enjoyed the feel of the cool night air against her skin, which was being basted with Jacob's sweat as he moved over her at a slightly increasing speed. She squeezed her eyes shut, trying to freeze this feeling into her mental and physical memory so that she would never, ever forget it.

A while later, Jacob picked up Sahara's slick, tingling body and carried her into the house so she wouldn't catch a cold. He got a blanket and they cuddled together on his huge, comfortable sage corduroy couch. Sahara didn't want to move, snuggled warmly under the thick blanket with her body molded against Jacob's. She rubbed her face against the faint hairs on his chest. She was still flying high, still able to feel him inside of her and his hands sliding up and down her thighs. Part of her couldn't believe what she had just done; slept with a man after only knowing him for a couple of months. But she wouldn't allow herself to regret it or start admonishing herself. The truth of the matter was, she had enjoyed it. Immensely. So much so that she was already looking forward to when they could do it again.

Sahara's eyes eventually drifted open and over to the big wood clock on the wall and was surprised that it was already almost ten o'clock. Charlie was keeping Rison while she was out and Sahara knew that it was time for her to go get her child. She reluctantly pushed away from Jacob, sitting up. He opened his eyes and looked at her questioningly.

"What's wrong? Where you going?" he asked, his voice low.

"It's getting late. I need to go pick up Rison."

"Aww..." he whined, gripping her waist with his strong, rough hand. "I understand why you would have to go but I sure as hell don't want you to. Do you have to leave *right* now? Rison's probably asleep already, right?"

Sahara bit her lip, the thought never occurring to her. She looked down at Jacob and knew that she didn't want to leave yet, either. Not any time soon. She couldn't engage in lovemaking like the kind he had put on her and then go to her cold bed alone.

"Excuse me a minute," she said, easing off of him and walking on slightly wobbly legs over to her purse, where she retrieved her cell phone. She went into the kitchen and dialed Charlie's number, shifting her weight from one leg to another and biting her lip nervously.

"Hello?"

"Hey, girl."

"Oh, hey Sahara! How was your date?"

"It was wonderful, but now I have a problem."

"What? What's wrong?"

"Well...I feel like such a moron for this, but when I got here I guess I was so anxious about the date with Jacob that I left my lights on and now my battery is dead. Plus, I'm practically out of gas. I guess I forgot to take care of that, too." She chuckled nervously.

Charlie giggled. "Oh, girl don't worry about that. I've done that myself more times than I can count. Just take your time. Do you need me to come get you?"

"Oh no," Sahara said quickly. "Jacob said he could take care of it for me, but it just might take a while, is all."

"No problem. If it gets to be too late, just come and get Rison in the morning. I don't have anywhere to be and she's already asleep, anyway. Don't even worry about it."

"Thank you so much, girl," Sahara said appreciatively, feeling only marginally guilty for lying to her friend. "I owe you one."

"You know I got you. I'm dead tired myself and was trying to sit up and not get too comfortable until you got here, but now I can go on and get in the bed. Just don't even worry about coming to get that child tonight 'cause in about thirty minutes I'm gonna be dead to the world."

"I feel you. I need to go lay down myself," Sahara responded. She didn't mention that she would be lying down on top of Jacob.

"All right then. Just call me in the morning."

"Thanks again, girl. Bye." Sahara hung up the phone and smiled. Charlie was such a good friend. Sahara wondered if she could've just told Charlie the truth and still gotten the same results, but shrugged off the thought. It was better this way, she reasoned to herself. She never liked to lie, but she didn't know if she was ready to let anybody know what had gone down between her and Jacob just yet, even though it was mainly Charlie who had encouraged her to not think so much and act on her feelings and follow her heart. That's what she had done and she had never felt as alive and free as she felt right then. It wasn't a feeling she was ready to let go of yet.

Putting her wants and needs first felt *nice*.

She returned to the living room, where Jacob was still stretched out on the couch. The blanket was only covering half of his body and it looked like he was struggling to stay awake.

Sahara smiled. She'd always heard men tended to fall asleep after a good round of sex.

Sensing her presence, his eyes opened. He reached for her. "So what's the deal, can you stay for a while?" he asked, his voice thick. He lightly grazed his trimmed nails up and down her toned calf.

"I can stay all night," Sahara responded, grinning.

"Yeah? Girl, you just made my night again. Come on in here," he said, lifting up the blanket for her to rejoin him under it. She crawled on top of him and he covered her with the soft tan-colored fabric, holding her close to him with his strong arms. Her chest was to his and she leaned up and gave him a lingering kiss. They wrapped their arms around each other as the kiss progressively deepened, pressing their bodies as close together as they could. Pretty soon, Jacob was getting up to get more condoms.

It was a night that Sahara couldn't get out of her head over the next couple of days. They'd had sex a few more times that evening, and Sahara realized she couldn't get enough of Jacob. At some point over the course of the night it had started to rain, and it was the perfect soundtrack when they made love on the living room floor and in his king-sized waterbed, and the perfect backdrop when they sexed against his sliding glass door. Their skin whistled as it slid against the cold glass, neither one of them caring that their clothes that they had left outside were getting drenched and possibly ruined in the pounding rain.

After she left Jacob's that next morning, all she could think about what was when she could be with him again. They talked daily, recalled their night together, both anticipating the next one. He had enjoyed it just as much as she had and if he had it his way, she would be at his house every night.

That would prove to be difficult, though, since Sahara had a date with Shannon the very next night. As usual, she had a wonderful time with him, but her mind kept drifting back to Jacob. That is, until the end of the evening when Shannon laid a kiss on her that made her forget about any and everything else. They did some very light petting, but that's about as far as it went physically. It was enough, though, to send Sahara home to masturbate for the first time in forever.

The high that she was on was only stalled slightly by a phone call from Kyle.

"Hey, Sahara," he greeted.

"Hello, Kyle."

"How's everything going?"

"Couldn't be better. What can I do for you?"

She certainly sounds chipper, Kyle thought to himself. "I was just wondering how come you don't call me anymore."

Is he serious? Sahara thought, amused. "I've tried to call you plenty of times, Kyle, but you never wanted to answer the phone. I quit trying after a while."

"When?" Kyle asked, confused. "I don't even *remember* the last time I got a call from you, Sahara."

"That's not my fault. I called."

"Then how come it's not in my call log or anything?"

"I don't know, Kyle. But I certainly don't have any reason to lie to you about calling, especially since each and every time I called it was because of Rison, not necessarily because I just wanted to talk to you."

"Damn, Sahara. You don't have to be so mean about it."

Sahara sighed. "I don't mean to sound harsh, Kyle, but I have tried to call you on numerous occasions, either because I needed you to watch Rison or she wanted to talk to you, and all I ever got was your voicemail. It was quite evident that you didn't have time to answer my calls so I stopped making them. I can't believe you're acting like you never got any one of my calls."

"I honestly didn't."

"Well, then I don't know what to tell you. Is that all you called for?"

Kyle didn't like Sahara brushing him off like this. He had gotten so used to her dropping everything for him that he still expected her to do it even though they were no longer together. "Yeah, that was it."

"All right then. I'll talk to you later." She hung up.

Sahara shook her head as she placed her phone on her desk. Kyle had some gall, calling her and acting like she hadn't been calling him endlessly. There was no way he didn't get any of those calls. She would like to think her name was in his phone by now, especially since she knew that was the only way he would be able to keep up with it. Kyle had never been good at remembering people's phone numbers by heart, no matter whose they were. He couldn't even recite his own mother's number from memory.

She giggled as she read an instant message from Tony as it popped up on her computer screen. He had started IMing her a short time ago and Sahara actually liked being able to communicate with him this way. As she typed in her reply to him, she wondered why it was that Kyle was acting all concerned about what she did all of a sudden. Ever since they split up, she had been trying to get him to spend more time with Rison, and to practically no avail. Did he have some kind of revelation? Or was he just finally starting to miss his daughter?

Dismissing those thoughts, she figured that her cousin Wanda had a hand in this somehow. Maybe *she* had been the one to make him see what a jackass he had been behaving like towards Rison and now he was finally starting to see the light. It would only make sense that he would listen to Wanda before he listened to her, since Wanda was apparently the one he was so in love with and she had significantly more influence over him. Sahara thought it was sweet of her cousin to convince Kyle to start putting in more effort towards Rison. It was sad that was what it took, but whatever got the job done was fine with Sahara. Rison wasn't asking about Kyle quite as much as she used to, but Sahara knew that didn't mean she didn't miss him. Charlie and Julia were just doing a really good job of keeping her mind off of her absentee father.

A couple of days later, when Sahara was at Tony's cleaning, he stayed in his office, saying he had a deadline. Part of Sahara was slightly disappointed because she had gotten used to Tony's constant attention, but she figured it was for the best. This way, she would be able to get her work done without either one of them being tempted into doing anything they probably didn't need to do.

When she went into the master bathroom, she knelt down to remove the green bath mat from the floor and immediately felt a pair of hands on her waist. She gasped and bolted upright, with Tony turning her to face him before she could do anything about it. The next thing she knew, his lips were on hers. She resisted a little at first, but found herself leaning into him and returning his kiss, her hands tentatively sliding up to grip his shoulders. Her head was screaming for her to stop kissing this man, that this was just *wrong*, that she knew better than to go here with a client, but her body wanted her to keep going. Tony was an extremely good kisser. It felt like he was making love to her mouth; she had never been kissed quite like this.

Before long, they were inching into his bedroom, their hands slowly exploring each other through the barriers of their clothing. They fell onto his full-size bed, Tony landing on top of her. His hands found their way under her shirt to grip her breasts and Sahara gasped. Her hips began to move against his, and pretty soon they were all-out grinding. Tony put his lips where his hands had been, flicking his tongue over Sahara's milk chocolate nipples, causing her to grunt and pant in a frustrated ecstasy. She wanted so much more but knew she was already probably going too far, so she just tried to get as close to Tony's bulging erection as she could through her work pants. His long black dreads fell around their faces as they panted against each other's mouths, each sharing the common goal to bring Sahara to orgasm. Not too long later, mission accomplished.

They didn't speak; Tony just peeled himself from Sahara's heaving body and went back into his office. Sahara gathered herself and wandered back into the bathroom to resume what she had gone in there for in the first place, although cleaning was now the last thing on her mind. She managed to get through it, though, and after she settled her business with Tony, she left. They hadn't said a word about what they had done, but she was really looking forward to the next time she was due over, hoping they would do it again.

She felt extremely invigorated, like a child who had gotten away with something that they knew was wrong and couldn't wait to see how much farther they could get the next time. She wanted that next time.

CHAPTER FIFTEEN

Wanda lounged on her and Kyle's bed, sliding her leg back and forth across the cream down comforter. She gently tossed Kyle's cell phone back and forth between her hands. Her lips curled into a sly smile.

She had erased Sahara's contact information from his phone weeks ago, knowing Kyle's ineptness when it came to memorizing numbers. She knew that he most likely wouldn't recognize Sahara's number when she called, and that he didn't answer unfamiliar numbers. That was the reason Sahara had been calling and getting no response. And Kyle hadn't even noticed that Sahara's name was missing from his contact list.

Wanda felt like she had to take some action. She and Kyle didn't seem to be moving anywhere. She had told him that she'd decided on a date for their wedding but he never even asked her what it was. After she had put it on him like she did after telling him, that seemed to be all he cared about. They never really discussed it anymore after that and now Wanda was getting restless. Whenever she alluded to it or tried to bring it up, he never seemed to give her his full attention. His mind was always on the situation with Sahara and Rison. And Wanda was more than fed up with it.

Part of her motivation for wanting to go ahead and set a date and get things moving on their wedding was that the sooner she and Kyle got married, the sooner she could quit her job. She hated going to work more and more with each passing day and would love nothing more than to tell those people to kiss her honeybuns, walk out, and never have to worry about going back. Kyle could make that happen if he would just focus on her instead of his ex-wife and his child.

It really burned Wanda that Sahara was messing up her program like she was, even though she wasn't doing it on purpose. That didn't matter. The fact was, thanks to her, Wanda wasn't getting what she wanted, and that just wouldn't fly. She could care less about who her goody-two-shoes cousin slept with, even though she was still pretty sure that women were not included on the roster. But on the slim chance that Kyle was right, she had to admit that she was slightly impressed. And even slightly relieved. If Sahara was into women now, Wanda wouldn't have to worry about her trying to get Kyle back.

All Wanda knew for certain was that if her little stunt of erasing Sahara's number from Kyle's phone didn't work as far as getting Kyle's attention back on her, then she would just have to try something else. And she already had an idea as to what that would be. Kyle no doubt wouldn't like it, but Wanda had every confidence that she would be able to get him to come around to her side. Just like she always did.

Kyle was trying to take a nap in the den, but he couldn't get to sleep. He knew Wanda was upstairs sulking about him still not discussing their wedding date, but she would just have to deal with it for the time being. His mind was on other things, namely getting back into the good graces of his daughter and even his ex-wife. He didn't want to be at odds with Sahara if he didn't have to be. They were going to have to deal with each other indefinitely so they might as well get along. He was sure Wanda could understand that. She wanted Rison with them as much as he did.

He missed Rison something terrible. It had been too long since he'd seen her and it was past time that he rectified that. Wanda had been right when she pointed out that he could have seen Rison at church if he wanted to. All he had to do was go downstairs to the nursery where she stayed during the service. But the thought never even occurred to him, and he didn't want to consider what that said about him.

He reached for his cell phone, but remembered he had left it upstairs. Not having the energy or desire to yell upstairs to Wanda to bring his phone down to him, partly because he didn't want to have to answer any questions about who it was he was calling, he eased off the sofa and tiptoed up to his office. He looked for the scrap of paper he had scribbled Sahara's number down on and tried to call her from his office line. He got no answer and couldn't help but wonder where she was and who she was with. He just couldn't help it.

It occurred to him to call Julia. He knew he probably wasn't too high on his ex-mother-in-law's list of favorite people, but he also knew it wasn't her nature to be rude. Only thing was, he had no idea what her number was off the top of his head so he had no choice but to go and get his cell phone. Thankfully, Wanda had drifted off to sleep and she slept like a log, so he just slipped in, got his cell phone from the night table, and slipped back out. Once he was back downstairs, he called Julia.

"Hello?"

"Julia, hello. It's Kyle."

There was a pause. "Hello, Kyle. How are you?"

"I'm good." He could tell that she was curious as to why he was calling her. He figured he should just skip the polite small talk and get right to the point. "I was trying to get in touch with Sahara but I can't seem to reach her. Do you happen to know where she is?"

"Yes, I do. She's at Tony's right now, I believe."

Kyle's ears burned. Toni? Was this *another* woman? What the hell was going *on* here? And where was Rison?? Julia didn't sound upset in the least about any of this. Was she trying to be understanding of her daughter's new lifestyle? Kyle always thought she let Sahara get away with too much.

"Oh, ahh...thanks, Julia. I guess I'll just try to catch her later then." Kyle had so many questions but he knew he couldn't very well ask Julia to answer them.

"You're welcome. You have a good evening."

"You, too. Bye." He disconnected the call and sank onto the couch, a frown marring his face. The more he thought about Sahara being with a different person seemingly every time he talked to her or someone who knew her, the more upset he became. Before long, he was furious. Sahara was just out of control.

He *had* to do something.

CHAPTER SIXTEEN

Sahara was having the time of her life. She had been a little apprehensive about dating more than one man at once but now that she was doing it, she was loving it.

Each man was wonderful in his own way. She especially enjoyed her time with Shannon. They just had so much in common and seemed to be the most compatible out of all the men she was interested in. And he never tried to put any moves on her or pressure her into taking things to another level physically. She knew he was attracted to her and she was most definitely attracted to him, and would be lying if she said she hadn't thought about going there with him. But she found that when she was with him, sex just wasn't what it was all about. She was interested in getting to know more about *him*, both inside and out. They could spend hours just talking. She just felt so at ease, so comfortable with Shannon.

And he showed her so much respect. Whenever she saw him after a long work day, he would always rub her feet and back and rake his hands through her hair, which she absolutely loved. He made her feel safe. She knew it sounded a little cheesy, but she really felt like a princess when she was around him.

As for Jacob, he was still rocking her world sexually. Just about every time she went to see him or even when she went out with him in public, she was always looking forward to when they could get to the point where they were both naked and bumping against each other. It seemed to be all she could think about when it came to him. Sure, she enjoyed his company and sincerely liked him as a person, but she wondered if her physical attraction to him exceeded everything else. She had to admit she really didn't want to think about it; she just wanted to enjoy it.

Then there was Tony. They were still kissing and grinding and licking on each other whenever she went over to clean his house, but still no sex. Every ounce of her body wanted to, but she just didn't feel comfortable having two sexual partners at once. She had to draw the line *somewhere*.

Between the three of them, Sahara was occupied just about every night of the week. Her social life was smokin' with a capital S. She still wasn't quite used to going out every night, and her body hadn't caught up to the increased pace. There were nights where she didn't get home until super late, if she even came home at all, and she wasn't getting as much sleep as she used to. As a result, she ended up having to reschedule an appointment here and there just so she would have more time to sleep.

Charlie was really helping her out with Rison. She either came over to Sahara's to babysit or kept Rison at her place, and Sahara couldn't have been more grateful. She was only following Charlie's advice, after all. She was putting herself first and having some long-overdue fun. And Charlie always insisted that she didn't mind keeping Rison at all; she loved her as if she were her own flesh-and-blood niece. That worked out really well for Sahara. Rison was spending a whole lot of time with Auntie Charlie and Sahara was getting her groove back. Even though Sahara knew she wasn't spending as much one-on-one time with Rison as she used to, she figured Charlie was showing her a good time. Everyone was happy.

As much fun as she was having, though, Sahara knew she couldn't keep letting things interfere with her business like she was. She had never been in the habit of doing that before and couldn't afford to make it a habit. But she was sure with her pretty much flawless track record up until this point, she had earned a little leeway. She had known a lot of her clients for years; they knew the kind of person she was. They could understand.

After she dropped Sahara off at preschool one morning, Sahara went into her office to get some neglected work done. She needed to order some supplies, return some emails, and pay some bills. Her marketing materials also needed replenishing and updating, as well as keeping track of the new referral program she had in place. She hadn't realized how behind she had gotten on things and really tried to buckle down and get things done. Occasionally her mind would wander to Shannon or Jacob or Tony, but after about an hour or so she started making some headway.

There was a knock at her door. Sahara frowned as she glanced towards the direction of the living room, wondering who it was that was just showing up at her place unannounced in the middle of the day. She finished typing out the email she was working on before she got up from her desk and headed into the living room to see who her midday visitor was.

The last thing she expected was to see her ex-husband standing there with another man.

CHAPTER SEVENTEEN

K yle tried to gauge Sahara's reaction as she perused the man standing next to him. He had brought him over to test her.

"Kyle," she ventured, still eyeing his friend curiously, "What's going on?"

"Hey, Sahara. Is this a bad time?"

She glanced over her shoulder and Kyle wondered if she had someone in the apartment with her. He tuned his ears in to listen for any sounds coming from her bedroom or anywhere, but he didn't hear anything. Not even a television. "Well, actually I was trying to get some work done..."

"This won't take too long. I wanted to introduce you to my friend Walter Mathis. He works with me at the firm and I've been telling him all about you. We were heading back to the office from a meeting across town and I thought we'd take a chance and see if you were home so I could introduce you two."

"Oh," Sahara said. He could tell she really wanted to get back to whatever she had been doing, but she didn't want to be impolite. He always liked that about her. She smiled sweetly and stuck out her hand. "How are you, Walter?"

"Very well, Sahara. It's nice to finally meet you. Kyle has been telling me a lot about you over the past couple of days."

"Is that right?" Sahara said, glancing at Kyle. She wondered why Kyle was talking her up so much to people, but she would save that question for when she and Kyle were alone.

"Oh yes. And now that I finally see you, I see why he couldn't keep your name out of his mouth."

Sahara blushed. Kyle noticed and was surprised that she was still so modest after all these years. "I'm flattered, Walter, thank you."

"I just think you two would get along great," Kyle chimed in. "Why don't you two go out sometime? I have a couple of tickets to that new play that's coming to town that I can give you. Wanda didn't want to go and I don't want them to go to waste."

Sahara looked at Kyle with slightly narrowed eyes. She didn't want to get an attitude in front of Walter, but she was angry with Kyle for putting her on the spot like this. She knew nothing about this man outside of his name, and Kyle expected her to go out with him just like that? With tickets to a play that the cousin he had cheated on her with and was now engaged to didn't want? He really, *really* had a lot of nerve.

They were both looking at her waiting for an answer. Even if she was interested, Sahara simply didn't have time to get involved with a fourth man. She looked at Walter, who was okay-looking but didn't spark any real interest in her, and gave a polite smile. "Walter, you seem like such a nice man and I enjoyed meeting you, but I just have a lot on my plate right now. Please don't take it personally."

Walter smiled what looked like a relieved smile and held up his hands. "Hey, no problem at all. It was nice meeting you, as well." He looked at Kyle and tapped him on the arm. "I'll be in the car, man."

He headed off down the driveway. Sahara gathered that he probably didn't really want to go out with her any more than she wanted to go out with him, but Kyle had probably badgered the poor man so much that he just came over out of duress.

Sahara waited until Walter was safely in the car and out of earshot before she lit into Kyle. "What is the big idea of you bringing some strange man over here out of the blue and expecting me to go out with him just on your recommendation? Have you lost your mind??"

Kyle was slightly taken aback by Sahara's anger. "What's the problem? He's a good guy; I just thought the two of you would hit it off. That's all."

Sahara put a hand on her hip. "What would make you think that I need your help with finding a date, Kyle?"

Kyle had to bite his tongue. He almost made a comment about her apparently very active social life that probably would have gotten him slapped. "This is really not that big of a deal, Sahara. I was just...I don't know. Trying to do something nice."

"Well, you don't need to worry about being nice to me. Be nice to Rison. Especially since she hardly even asks about you anymore."

Kyle's heart stopped. "Are you serious?"

"I'm very serious."

Kyle didn't know what to say. He never thought things would get to this point.

"You need to quit being so worried about what *I'm* doing and get reacquainted with your daughter," Sahara said, her voice softening slightly. She could see how hurt he was by her announcement. But it was the truth and definitely something he needed to know. Rison spent so much time with Charlie and Julia that she rarely even mentioned Kyle's name anymore.

"All right, Sahara. Thanks for letting me know that," Kyle muttered. He glanced over his shoulder towards the car and reached into the inside pocket of his dark blue suit. "Here, let me give you one of Walter's cards..."

Sahara couldn't believe his nerve. Not only had he apparently not listened to a word she said, but even after what she just told him, he was *still* trying to hook her up with someone whom she had already said she had no interest in.

"Kyle..." she sighed, shaking her head. "Just...just go away." She closed the door in his face.

Kyle just stood there with the card in his hand looking at the apartment number on Sahara's door. He couldn't believe she had shut him down like that. To him, it only solidified his suspicions. Walter was a great catch; handsome, had a great job, a gentleman, all that. But Sahara still wasn't interested. To Kyle, she wasn't interested in Walter because he wasn't a woman.

Kyle just couldn't let go of this supposed issue with Sahara. As much as he tried to dismiss it as not his problem and put it out of his mind, he always strayed back to it. He was constantly thinking about what she might be doing and who she might be going out with any particular night. It was crazy. On a couple of occasions, he would even cruise by her apartment in the hopes of catching another glimpse of the end or beginning of one of her dates. He wanted to call Julia and grill her for information. He even thought about taking Rison out for the day and gently probing her for answers. Even though he knew that was crazy and totally inappropriate, he just couldn't help himself.

He told himself it was out of concern for his daughter that he was so immensely consumed with Sahara's love life. Of course he was concerned with who was being brought around

Rison. He wanted to know what she was being told, how she was being treated, how she liked these people, where she was when Sahara was going out on all these dates, everything. And he felt like he had a right to know all this.

And not just for Rison's sake...also for Sahara's somewhat, too. He still cared about her, after all. The last thing he wanted was for her to do something drastic or foolish because she was still distraught and trying to get over him. Part of him still felt responsible for her, just like he had pretty much ever since they met.

When Kyle met Sahara back in high school, he thought she was gorgeous but knew that she was a particularly quiet and somewhat demure shy girl who didn't seem to get out very much. Even though she looked as good as she did, it was clear she didn't have a lot of confidence. Kyle was drawn to her because she was so incredibly different from all the other girls, especially the ones with her kind of looks. She was so nice, sometimes to a fault, that he couldn't help but approach her. Usually the girls that pretty hardly gave him the time of day, not considering him *cool* enough, but Sahara took to him immediately. She viewed his intelligence as an asset instead of a flaw. She actually wanted to study with him, and often went to him when she needed help or advice with something. Kyle was flattered that she valued his opinion so much and found himself wanting to look out for her in any and every way he could.

Before he knew it, Kyle was in love with Sahara. Maybe not *madly* in love, but more than enough to stay with her and build a life with her. He just thought she was too good of a woman to pass up. Women who had her looks *and* her good attitude were rare. And besides that, she was totally committed to and supportive of him. He appreciated that, and part of him felt like he owed her for it. So he tried to take the best care of her that he could, providing her with everything that she needed, especially after they got married. He wanted to be the best husband that he could to her, because he felt that she simply deserved it.

And even after things started to fall apart, he still wanted to do right by her, providing her with more than the judge-appointed child support and alimony. Even though he was now committed to Wanda, he still felt a responsibility to Sahara, and not just because she was the mother of his child. He genuinely still cared about her.

This fact was causing a problem for Wanda, because it was very obvious. She did *not* like at all that her man so still so concerned about his ex-wife. There was something wrong with that to her. To her, after he left Sahara to be with her, *she* should have been his main focus. Otherwise, why the hell was he with her? He could've just stayed with Sahara if she was still going to be getting this much of his attention.

Even Wanda's attempts at seducing Kyle weren't as effective as they once were. Usually, all she had to do was throw on one of her g-strings or touch him a certain way and he forgot about everything else. Now, it wasn't so easy. He always seemed distracted. Even the sight of her on the floor doing one of her famous Chinese splits didn't get to him like it used to. It barely caused him to stir. This was not going to work at *all*.

And they still had yet to really discuss their wedding. Kyle probably hadn't even thought about it. That was a fact that bothered her extremely. She was beginning to wonder if he even still wanted to marry her, and her plan was hitting a major snag. The end result was always supposed to be to end up as Mrs. Kyle Johnson. And now it was looking like that might not happen. Kyle was losing focus.

She had to do something to make him get it back.

CHAPTER EIGHTEEN

Jacob held Sahara close to him as they lay together in his bed. They had been making love for the past hour and he was getting more and more used to having her there with him.

"That was great," Sahara panted, running a hand through her damp raven tresses.

"Always is," Jacob confirmed. He kissed the top of her head.

They were silent for a while. Sahara still loved the sex between her and Jacob. She no longer felt guilty about their sexual relationship, especially since it seemed like every time they got together, he showed her something new. He always kept her guessing. Sometimes their sessions were slow and meticulous, and sometimes they were wild and aggressive and even messy. Sahara loved it; she loved Jacob's range. Sometimes she wondered if she actually loved *him*, but wasn't sure. She certainly loved spending time with him and the sex they shared, but she didn't know if it went any further than that. Maybe it could in time, but it wasn't there yet.

"Sahara," Jacob said softly, gently squeezing her shoulder.

"Hmm?"

"I have to be honest with you about something."

Sahara opened her eyes as a mild sense of dread coursed through her. "Yeah?"

"I know you said you weren't ready for a relationship or anything like that, but I'm honestly getting to the point where I just want you all to myself."

"Really?" Sahara hadn't been expecting that.

"Yeah. It's just that the more time I spend with you, the more I get into you. You're the kind of woman I can see myself with long-term."

Sahara smiled because she was flattered, though she didn't quite return his feelings.

She sat up and looked at him, taking his hand in both of hers and holding it to her bare chest. "Jacob, I care for you so much. I really and truly do. But to be honest, I'm still not ready to be exclusive to anyone right now. Can you understand that?"

Jacob sighed. He had kind of expected her to say that but was hoping she would surprise him. "Yeah, I can."

"I'm so sorry. Do you want me to leave?"

"No, no of course not," he quickly responded. He brought her hand up to his lips and kissed it, giving her a sad smile. "I know you want to take things slow, as far as relationships go. I knew that from the beginning. My feelings for you are deepening but I knew what I was getting into when you and I first started hanging out. I guess I can only hope that one day you'll feel the same way about me that I'm starting to feel about you."

Sahara reached out and touched his handsome face. "I really hate to disappoint you, Jacob, 'cause I like you more than I can say. But I just don't want to lead you on."

"I know. And I appreciate that. You've been honest with me from the jump and I guess that's all I can ask for."

Sahara smiled. She wanted to be honest with the men she was seeing because she knew how much it hurt when Kyle wasn't honest with her when they were together. "So, we're good, then?"

"Yeah, girl, we're good," he said, looking at her and smiling. He pulled her back to him.

Sahara laid her head on his chest, glad that he understood where she was coming from. As much as she liked Jacob, she wondered if she could really be with him long-term. For some reason, she felt that Jacob would eventually get bored with her, or even vice versa. That might be because they had taken things to a physical level so quickly; they didn't *really* get to know each other first. And when she *did* decide to get with someone exclusively, she didn't want to get involved in any relationships that she didn't think would last. And even though she had been in only one serious relationship, even she knew that those based on sex didn't usually last long.

In all honesty, Sahara thought that if she ended up with anyone it would be Shannon. He seemed to be the one the most willing to take his time with her and really get to know her as a person before they did anything physical. And she appreciated that. She felt no pressure whatsoever, and that allowed her to relax with him. With Tony and Jacob, their physical attraction towards her was evident from the beginning. And she couldn't necessarily penalize them for that because it was totally reciprocated. She had wanted them as much as they wanted her, and she acted on it.

But there was something to be said about a man that wanted to get to know her mind first, even though he clearly appreciated the body. It made him stand out. And overall, she just liked how she felt with Shannon.

Later on that evening, Sahara was making dinner while Rison practiced writing her letters in her room. She was on the phone with Charlie, the phone lodged between her ear and shoulder, chopping vegetables for a salad as a meat loaf cooked in the oven. She was telling Charlie about Kyle's misguided attempt to set her up.

"Honestly, Charlie, I can't tell you how surprised I was when Kyle showed up at my door with that man," she said, gathering the cucumbers she had just sliced and dropping them into the bowl of lettuce beside her. "Kyle really has a lot of nerve."

"Girl, that shouldn't be anything new," Charlie responded. "You didn't like the guy he brought over?"

"He was okay; seemed nice enough. It wasn't really about that, though. I just didn't like how Kyle put me on the spot like he did. He shows up out of the blue, with some man I've never seen and expects me to go out with him just because he says he's a nice guy."

"Yeah, I can see how you would be put off by that."

"And what's worse, he offered us tickets to some play that he had gotten for Wanda but she apparently didn't want. For him to even tell me that was just plain stupid. How could he think I would want those?"

"You're kidding," Charlie gasped. "He obviously wasn't thinking."

"He couldn't have been."

"I'm wondering why Kyle is trying to set you up with anybody in the first place," Charlie mused. "It's almost like he's feeling guilty or something and is trying free his conscience."

"Well, if that's what it is, he needs to rethink his methods. I'm not the one he needs to be concerned so much about. Mama even told me that he called her asking where I was a few nights ago."

"Are you serious? For what?"

"I don't think he really said what it was he wanted with me. He was probably just trying to be nosey. Ever since he called me that time that you and I were out to dinner and he thought you were a man, he's been calling me a lot more and trying to subtly fish for information about who I'm with."

"I'm not all that surprised about that, though," Charlie said. "Kyle seems to want to have his cake and eat it, too. He wanted to leave you but still have a say in what you do. He probably didn't even expect you to get with anyone else. Didn't you tell me he was your first?"

"Yeah," Sahara said, scooping up the chopped celery.

"He probably feels like he has some kind of claim to you."

Sahara thought about that. It made sense. That might explain the way Kyle had been acting lately.

"I had been thinking that Kyle trying to set me up with Walter was his way of trying to keep tabs on me," Sahara stated. "Since he works with the guy all day he would have plenty of opportunity to pump him for information or even coach him on where he thinks we should go or what he thinks we should do. I wouldn't even put it past him to 'accidentally' show up on one of the dates, trying to spy. I'm glad I turned the guy down."

"Yeah, me too."

"I was sure to let Kyle know that I don't need any help in finding dates. Speaking of that, are you still keeping Rison for me this weekend? Shannon wants to take me to that bed-and-breakfast that he co-owns."

"Yeah..." Charlie answered hesitantly. It was clear she had something else to say and Sahara waited patiently for her to get it out.

"Sahara, you know I love you and Rison and I have no problem watching her, but I think you need to start spending a little more time with her."

Sahara was getting the salad dressing from the refrigerator, but froze at Charlie's words. "What?"

"Rison needs more time with you, Sahara," Charlie continued gently. "Especially since she hardly sees Kyle. I'm glad that you're going out and enjoying yourself, but you should really make some time in your schedule for your daughter, too. She needs you."

Sahara found herself getting agitated. Who was Charlie to say something like that to her? She didn't even have any kids.

"I think I know what my daughter needs, Charlie," she retorted with an edge in her voice, snatching the dressing from the refrigerator and slamming the door shut.

"Sahara, don't take offense to this," Charlie pleaded quickly. "You know you're my girl, but I have to be honest with you. I think you're getting caught up in this new social life of yours a little too much. All I'm trying to do is remind you to not forget about your daughter, because she's still going to be here even after all these men aren't."

"Well, thank you so much for your advice, *Charlie*," Sahara snapped sarcastically. "Especially since *you're* the main one that was pushing me to go out and meet all these men. Everybody seems to have some kind of problem with *me* having a good time. No, Sahara is just supposed to sit in the house with her daughter all the time and never go anywhere, right?"

"Of course not, Sahara. You know that's not what I'm saying at all. But you have to find a balance. *Rison* is the one you're supposed to be obligated to, not the men in your life."

"Look, if you don't want to babysit for me anymore, just say so. I'll get my mother to do it."

"Sahara-"

"Good night," Sahara cut her off, ending the call. She was fuming.

She finished the salad and took the meat loaf out of the oven, trying to calm herself down. She thought Charlie had some nerve, implying that she was neglecting Rison. It's not like she went out every night of the week. She saw Rison plenty; they lived together, after all. She picked her up from school and helped her with her homework most days. It might not have been like it used to be, with Sahara home most of the time when she wasn't working, but things weren't that different. Sahara was sure that her little girl understood that she was just a little busy but she still loved her.

She was *nothing* like Kyle.

Sahara called Rison for dinner. After they blessed the food and began eating, Rison asked, "Mommy, can we go to the zoo this weekend?"

"I'll see if Grandma will take you, sweetie. Mommy has something to do."

"No! I want *you* to take me!"

"Well, I can't this weekend, Rison. You either go with her or you don't go at all."

Rison pouted, pushing her food around on her plate. "You're always gone, Mommy. I want *you* to take me somewhere," she muttered.

Sahara tried to keep her temper in check. First Charlie and now Rison. It was like she was supposed to live for everyone else except herself. Was she really supposed to feel bad for wanting to put herself first for a change?

All she wanted was for everyone to understand that she was just trying to enjoy herself for once. What was so wrong with that?

CHAPTER NINETEEN

"Sahara, I want you to come over here *today*," Julia said emphatically.

"Why? What's wrong?"

"I need to speak with you and it's very important. It can't wait. So I don't care what you have to do, but make sure you're at this house before the day ends." Julia's voice was stern.

Sahara was puzzled as she got off the phone. Julia hardly ever took that tone with her. *It must be something serious,* Sahara mused as she looked over her schedule.

She also ran over in her mind what she might have done wrong and couldn't come up with anything. Her curiosity was piqued, although she was also a little nervous. Her mother didn't get upset with her very often but it sure sounded like she was upset with her now.

She was supposed to go over to Tony's but it looked like she was going to have to reschedule. She dialed Tony's number, her mind still on what it was her mother could be upset with her about.

"Well, this is a nice surprise," Tony greeted her. "How are you, my queen?"

Sahara smiled. He started calling her that after the first night they kissed and she kind of liked it. "I'm good, Tony. I'm calling because I'm gonna have to reschedule our appointment tonight. There's some kind of issue with my mother."

"Is she all right?"

"I think she's fine, but I just need to go over there. She was very adamant about it."

"I understand. It's no problem. But you know you owe me, right?" he asked, his voice dropping.

Sahara's smile widened. Ever since that first night they kissed, they'd been doing that and a lot more every time she went over there. They still hadn't had sex, but they had done just about everything short of it. Sahara really looked forward to her time there. She would clean the house first, and then they would enjoy each other. They kissed, they grinded, they explored each other's bodies. Usually afterward, Sahara would get right up and leave. They didn't spend a lot of time talking.

Once Sahara got to Julia's, her mother wasted no time getting down to business.

"I am very concerned, Sahara," Julia said once they were both seated in the living room. "I think your social life is getting a little out of control."

That was the last thing Sahara expected. She didn't even think her mother knew a lot about it. Had someone told her? "Why do you say that?"

"I've been getting some calls," Julia said. "Some of your clients have been wondering why you've been cancelling so many appointments lately."

"Are you serious?" Sahara marveled, embarrassed. She felt like a child who had been tattled on.

"I'm very serious. They said it's not like you at all and wondered if you were ill or something. I really didn't know what to tell them, Sahara."

Sahara blushed and looked down at her hands. "I don't know what to say, Mama..."

"These people are my friends, Sahara," Julia continued, looking right into her daughter's eyes. "I referred them to you.

It partially reflects on me when you behave irresponsibly. Now *what* is going on with you?"

Sahara looked at her mother timidly. She had never liked being reprimanded by her, which was part of the reason she tried so hard to stay out of trouble. Now, as an adult, she still tried to stay on her mother's good side. Julia never really raised her voice, but she had a crisp, stern way of speaking when she was ticked off that made you feel about two feet tall.

"Mama, I'm sorry if I've embarrassed you. But I didn't think things were all that bad. I've just been trying to enjoy myself like everyone's been telling me I should do."

"Don't try to make it seem like this is anyone else's fault other than your own," Julia scolded. "We might've told you to go out a little more and have some fun, but I'm sure no one said for you to become slack on your business or start neglecting your daughter. Did we?"

"No ma'am," Sahara responded shyly.

"I think you've been enjoying the attention of these men a little too much. And it should be said that if these men were about anything, *they* would suggest that you spend a little more time with your child. Am I correct?"

"Yes, ma'am."

Sahara didn't mention that Shannon actually *did* ask if they were going out too much and if he was interfering with her time with Rison, but Sahara had ensured him that he wasn't. She wasn't about to admit that to her mother, though. Especially since now that she thought about it, it was kind of embarrassing. It was like she had been afraid she would lose Shannon's interest if she admitted to needing or wanting more time at home with her child, even though she really knew better than that.

"I haven't seen you in church the last couple of Sundays, either," Julia continued. "Are you too busy for God now, too?"

Sahara's face was on fire. She had been missing church lately, mostly because she would be too tired from whatever she did Saturday night and the prior week and wanted to catch up on some sleep. One time, it was because she was over at Jacob's after having spent the night and they just wanted to spend the day together alone.

"I wouldn't put it that way," Sahara muttered in a low voice. She played with her fingers in her lap. "I guess I don't really have an excuse for that."

"I'm glad, because there isn't one," Julia stated. She got up and sat next to Sahara on the couch, placing her hand on her knee. She softened her tone when she said, "Baby, you've been through a lot and it's understandable that you want to have something for yourself. But you simply cannot forget about your responsibilities. You might feel like one, but you're not a teenager anymore. There *has* to be a balance."

That was the same thing Charlie had tried to tell me, Sahara thought. *And I didn't even want to listen to her.*

"Maybe I got a little carried away," Sahara finally admitted. "But I've just been so angry and hurt by what Kyle did to me, and I guess I was just trying to put my own needs first for a while."

"Well let me ask you this...who is putting Rison's needs first? Because between Kyle's behavior and the way you've been acting lately, that little girl feels like neither of her parents loves her."

Tears came to Sahara's eyes at her mother's words. She was finally starting to see the error of her ways. She knew it had to be pretty bad for her mother to even get involved, since she usually didn't give her opinion about Sahara's business until she was asked for it. But Sahara had gotten a little out of control and something had to be done.

Julia took Sahara into her arms and held her lovingly, stroking her hair away from her face. "Baby, there's nothing wrong with dating and going out and enjoying yourself. Nothing at all. But you're a single mother with her own business and a four-year-old child who misses her parents. You can't let some man come before that. The *right* man will know and accept his place in your life, but you have to let him know what that place is. Your priorities are in serious need of rearranging."

She was right. Sahara knew she was right.

On her way home, she thought about her situation. She'd been having so much fun, finally enjoying this new phase of her life, but had pushed her child to the backburner in the process. She recalled how she responded when Rison asked her to take her to the zoo. All Sahara had been concerned about what going away with Shannon and wanted to immediately pawn her off on Julia, even getting upset with Rison for insisting that she, her own mother, take her instead of someone else. As if she was wrong for that. Sahara wanted to kick herself. She needed to reassure Rison that she was the top priority in her life.

She went over to Charlie's to pick up Rison. She was anxious to get her daughter home and spend some long-overdue quality time together, as well as having that much needed talk with her. They could order a pizza and watch one of those Disney movies that Rison loved so much.

Sahara's plan hit a snag, though, when she got to Charlie's and Rison didn't want to leave.

"I want to stay with Auntie Charlie," she stated emphatically, holding onto Charlie's leg.

Sahara was shocked. That was the first time Rison had ever refused to go with her anywhere and she couldn't deny that it hurt. "Rison, come on. We're can go home and do something really fun-"

"No!"

"Rison!" Charlie scolded sternly, kneeling down and taking Rison by the arms. "You know better than to speak to your mother like that. Right?"

Rison hung her head. "Yes, ma'am."

"I want you to apologize to her right now."

"I'm sorry," Rison said to Sahara, briefly glancing at her. She looked back at Charlie for her approval. She evidently didn't like Charlie to be upset with her.

"All right," Charlie said, her voice softening. "Now go and get your things so you can go home with your mother. And do it quickly. You can come over here another time."

"Yes, ma'am," Rison said again, heading off to get her bag. Sahara just stood there, dumbfounded.

Charlie stood and looked at Sahara. She could tell Sahara was upset by what had just happened.

"I know that had to hurt," she empathized. "Just talk to her when y'all get home; she's upset but I'm sure you can get back on her good side. Can I get you anything?"

Sahara just shook her head. She still couldn't believe that Rison was listening to Charlie more than she was listening to her. When had things gotten to this point?

When Sahara and Rison got home, Sahara tried to sit her down and talk to her about what had been going on. But Rison didn't want to hear it.

"I want to go live with Auntie Charlie or Grandma!" she yelled before Sahara could even get a word out.

Sahara was shocked. "What? Honey, why would you say something like that?"

"You and Daddy don't love me no more. I don't want to live with you!" She ran into her room.

CHAPTER TWENTY

Sahara wiped away the tears that streamed down her face with the back of her hand. She had been in her room crying ever since Rison told her she didn't want to live with her anymore.

Rison had never, ever spoken to her in such a manner. She had always been such a sweet and respectful little girl. Ever since she was born, she was Sahara's little sidekick. They had an extra strong bond since Sahara was a stay-at-home mother for most of her life and Rison was the only child. Wherever Sahara was, Rison was right there with her. And that's how Sahara loved it. She loved how Rison wanted to be wherever she was, especially since she knew that would probably only last so long. Sahara wanted to relish every moment of her little girl's undying devotion. She could kick herself for messing that up.

She had no idea things had gotten so bad. All she had wanted to do was a have a little fun and be carefree for a while. She didn't mean to neglect her little girl in the process. But apparently that's exactly what she had done. Charlie tried to warn her but she hadn't wanted to hear it. All she had cared about was what *she* had wanted.

For all the penalizing she had been doing of Kyle, she hadn't been acting much better recently.

She wondered if she should call Kyle and let him know what was going on. Maybe he would have some suggestions. At the very least, she knew they needed to put their heads together and find a solution to this. Their daughter was feeling abandoned by them both and it was past time they dealt with it.

But once again, when she tried to call Kyle, she got no answer. After two calls, she gave up, frustrated. For whatever reason, he *still* wasn't answering her calls. This was getting ridiculous. How was it that he was always calling her, but always unavailable when she tried to call him?

She was just lying on her bed, looking mindlessly up at the ceiling when she heard a hard knock on the door. Thinking it might be Kyle on another one of his impromptu visits, she quickly got up to answer it. For once she would be glad to see him because they really did need to talk.

But it wasn't Kyle at the door. It was his fiancé.

Sahara slowly opened the door, a slight frown on her face. She fully laid eyes on her cousin Wanda for the first time in what seemed like forever. She was one of the absolute last people Sahara wanted to see right then and she didn't try to make it seem otherwise.

"What are you doing here, Wanda?"

"Now is that any way to greet your cousin, Sahara-Beara?" Wanda asked, using Sahara's childhood nickname.

Sahara crossed her arms and shot Wanda a stern glare. Her cousin stood there looking all prim, dressed in a form-fitting white short-sleeved blouse and beige skirt that stopped at her knees, her large breasts and ample bottom straining against the fabric. A purse hung over her shoulder and her hair smelled freshly done.

"Wanda, I am not in the mood today, just let me tell you," Sahara warned. "And I really do not appreciate you just showing up at my place unannounced."

"Would you have welcomed me over if I had called?"

"I might've at least been more receptive than I am right now."

"Sahara, I just need to talk to you for a minute. I'm already here; it would be rude not to let me in."

"Well I guess I'll just have to be rude, then," Sahara said coldly, starting to close the door.

"Sahara!" Wanda called out, blocking the door with her hand. She wasn't used to all of this attitude from her usually-polite cousin. "Look, I don't know what your issue is today, but don't take it out on me. Is this how you want to treat family?"

Sahara gave her a look that could melt steel and Wanda actually took a step back. "You *really* don't want to go there with me."

Wanda realized she might have hit a nerve so she tried a different approach. "Look, it's about Kyle. You would *really* want to hear this, Sahara."

Sahara sighed. Since her curiosity was piqued very slightly at the mention of Kyle's name, especially since she had been trying to reach him unsuccessfully, she opened the door wider and went to sit on the couch.

Wanda came in and closed the door before taking a seat in the armchair facing Sahara. She didn't think it wise to sit next to her on the couch. "I'm gonna get right to the point, cuz-"

"Do *not* call me that."

"You are still my cousin, Sahara, whether you like it or not."

"Not as far as I'm concerned."

Wanda was a little taken aback by that. She wondered when Sahara had gotten all this backbone. "Well, be that as it may, I'm here and we both know I'm not going anywhere, as far as *Kyle* is concerned. I'm not trying to throw anything in your face, but honestly, Sahara, you are messing up my household."

Sahara's face screwed up. "Excuse me?"

"Frankly, who you choose to date or whatever is your business, but for whatever reason Kyle is so worried about it that it's coming between us."

Sahara shrugged. She hoped Wanda wasn't expecting any sympathy from her because she had another thing coming. "So what am I supposed to do about that? I've already told Kyle that who I date is none of his concern."

"Yeah? Well, I need you to tell him again. And again and again until he gets it. Because thanks to this little...*situation*, he won't get things going on our wedding. I need for you to talk to him."

Sahara wanted to laugh in her face. "You're kidding, right?"

"Absolutely not."

"You've gotta be."

"Look, Sahara. If you want to do, you know, what it is you do, then fine. I'm certainly not judging you. I've even tried it once or twice. But the honest truth of the matter is that it's coming between me and Kyle, who, like it or not, is with *me* now. Let's just be adults about all this and work together so we can all be happy and get what we want."

Sahara couldn't believe her ears. Apparently Kyle had been telling Wanda all about what he thought about Sahara's social life. Well, whether he approved of her dating more than one man at a time or not, it was not her problem that his being so worried about it was causing problems between him and Wanda.

Wanda had to admit that her cousin looked good. She had taken good care of herself over the years, even though Wanda had to grudgingly admit that Sahara never really had to do much. She was a natural beauty. Wanda always wished she had legs like Sahara's. Not to mention her long jet-black hair, pretty eyes and long, toned torso. It was too bad she wanted to waste all that on other women.

"It's about time for you to leave, Wanda," Sahara said, getting up and heading for the door.

Wanda sighed and stood up, slinging her purse over her shoulder. She sauntered over to the door and stopped in front of Sahara.

"There's one more thing I think you should know."

"What?" Sahara asked, rolling her eyes.

"After we're married, Kyle plans to petition for custody of Rison."

Sahara's eyes snapped to her. "What did you say?"

"Kyle wants custody of Rison and he's been planning on getting it after we're married. He thinks that our household will be more stable for her seeing as how there'll be two parents with more income, not to mention, you know, your little *experiment*."

Sahara's mouth fell open. That bastard!

Wanda reached out and put a hand on her arm. "Just so you know, I'm on *your* side on this. Rison has been through enough and doesn't need to be shuffled between houses. She needs her mother." She cast a sympathetic glance at her cousin before stepping outside and sashaying to her car.

Sahara closed the door behind her slowly. Kyle was scheming to get custody of her little girl?

So, after cheating with her cousin, divorcing her with no remorse whatsoever and then getting engaged to Wanda before the ink was even dry on the papers, now he planned on taking Rison away from her, too. He was just going to spring all of this on her, apparently, out of the blue. That sneaky, conniving son-of-a-bitch.

Well, if he thought she was going to take this lying down, he needed to think again. Sahara went to check on Rison, who was sound asleep on her bed, before she rushed to her phone and dialed Kyle's number. The only number she had for him was his cell number, since he had never given her his new home number and she'd never had his office number since he never thought she needed to know it. Once again she got no answer, so she began blowing his phone up, calling him repeatedly with no breaks in between. She was going to get through to this man one way or another, even if she had to call him a thousand times in a row.

After what seemed like the thousandth time, Kyle answered, his voice angry. "Who the hell is this?"

"Who do you think it is, you bastard?"

"Sahara?"

"Are you really gonna act like you didn't know it was me?"

"No I didn't know it was you. Your name didn't come up on my ID."

"Yeah. Right."

"I'm serious. I'm just now noticing that your name isn't in my phone."

"So it's like that, huh? You wanna erase all my contact information like you don't even know me on top of everything else, huh?"

"Sahara, I promise you I didn't do this on purpose. I'm almost positive that I didn't erase you out of my phone."

"So who did, then?"

"I really couldn't tell you."

"Look," Sahara sighed, "You and I need to talk and we need to do it quickly."

"I agree," he concurred. "I have a couple of meetings I absolutely cannot miss but I can come over right after those."

"Fine," Sahara confirmed. That would give her plenty of time to calm down. "See you then."

CHAPTER TWENTY-ONE

When Kyle arrived at Sahara's a few hours later, Sahara didn't want to waste any time getting things out in the open. Before she got into what Wanda had told her, though, she thought it best to address what was going on with Rison first.

"We need to talk about Rison," she said. "She's very unhappy right now. Between the two of us, she's been feeling very neglected and abandoned and now she says she doesn't even want to live with me anymore."

Kyle's eyebrows shot up. "Did something happen that I should know about?"

"I can admit that I haven't been the most attentive mother lately," Sahara acknowledged, looking down at her hands. "I've been going out a lot and spending more time enjoying my social life than spending time with Rison. I didn't even realize how bad it had gotten until today."

"I see," Kyle said, a slight frown marring his forehead. He was angry at Sahara but knew he had to check himself somewhat because he hadn't been doing what he was supposed to do, either. He hadn't spent any time with his daughter in too long, and he couldn't even say he had a good reason for that.

But he thought it was past time he confronted Sahara about this new social life of hers. It was obviously causing problems with their daughter and plus, he really just wanted to ask her what the heck she was thinking.

"Sahara, we need to talk about this whole lifestyle of yours."

Sahara was a little puzzled by his choice of words. "My *lifestyle*? I would hardly call it a lifestyle, Kyle. All I've been doing is going out on a few too many dates."

"That's all, huh? Well, my issue isn't necessarily the amount of dates you've been on. It's who the dates have been *with*."

Sahara sighed in frustration, throwing her hands up. "Why in the world do you care so much about who I've been dating? You don't even know anything about them, anyway."

"I know enough. More than you seem to think I do."

"Oh really? What have you been doing, spying on me?"

Kyle felt his face flush. She couldn't know about that. "Nevertheless-"

"And since we're on the subject of knowing more than the other thinks, let me tell you something that *I* know," Sahara cut him off. "Your woman came to see me today and she had some very interesting information for me."

Kyle sat up straight. "Wanda came to see you? For what?"

"To tell me that you're planning on getting custody of Rison after you two are married."

"What?!" Kyle was furious. He couldn't believe that Wanda had gone behind his back and told Sahara about that. She knew full well it was supposed to be a secret!

"Yep. She told me all about it. Seeing as how you apparently weren't going to tell me until after you filed the papers. That seems to be some kind of trend with you."

Kyle knew she was referring to how he had had divorce papers drawn up before Sahara even knew he wanted a divorce.

"Well, Wanda shouldn't have told you that. It wasn't her place. But I'm not gonna lie and say it isn't true because it is. I *do* want Rison to live with us after we're married."

"Over my dead body."

Kyle was a little surprised by her statement. He hadn't expected her to be happy about it but he had never heard Sahara say such a thing. She was just changing all the way around.

"Look, Sahara. Rison needs to be in a stable household with two parents with stable careers. Not in a single-parent lesbian household that's supported by a fledging cleaning business."

Sahara looked at him quickly, frowning. What had he just said?

"You wanna back that up a little bit, Kyle? What the heck do you mean, *lesbian* household? I am not a lesbian!"

"Oh please, Sahara. Let's quit pretending here. I already know about all the women."

"*What* women?"

"I saw you with some woman outside when I had come over one night to see Rison. Y'all were hugging and laughing and kissing each other on the cheek and stuff. I was so put off by that little scene that I just drove off. Not to mention you going out on all these dates with people like Shannon and Toni. Yeah, I know about all that!"

Sahara just looked at him.

"With all sincerity, Sahara, I apologize for driving you to this," Kyle continued, taking her hand. "I knew my leaving you for Wanda would hurt but I had no *idea* you would just give up on men altogether. Maybe you should get some help; go see a counselor or something. It shouldn't be too late to get you back from the dark side. This might just be a little phase you're going through brought on by the grief of losing me."

Sahara couldn't hold it in. She finally understood what he was talking about and burst out laughing right in his face.

"Kyle, you *idiot*!" she sputtered in between guffaws. Kyle looked at her like she was losing her mind. After a couple of minutes, she was finally able to compose herself somewhat. She wiped the tears streaming down her face with the back of her hand. She couldn't believe Kyle had actually thought she was a lesbian. He *actually* believed that she had been so distraught over him that she turned to women.

Sahara's stomach was hurting, she was laughing so much. And every time she looked at him and saw how serious he was, she laughed harder.

"Sahara..."

"Kyle, I am not a lesbian. The woman you saw me with was probably Charlie, who is just a friend I met at church. And as for Shannon and Tony, they're both men."

Kyle looked at her skeptically, wondering if she was making this all up. He figured it could make sense. And Sahara had never been a dishonest person. Why had he automatically jumped to the conclusion that she was a lesbian? Just because he had seen her hug another woman? No wonder she was laughing at him. He felt ridiculous.

"So that's why you haven't been answering my calls? Because you were upset when you thought I was a lesbian?" Sahara asked, calming down.

"Well I admit I was upset about that but its like I told you, your name wasn't in my phone. I don't know why its not; I'm pretty sure I didn't erase it."

"Then who did?"

Kyle couldn't answer, although there was only one other person who had direct access to his phone. And he would get to the bottom of this as soon as she got home from work.

• • • •

KYLE DIDN'T EXPECT to see Wanda home when he got home about an hour later.

"What are you doing home already?" he asked her, trying to keep the attitude out of his voice. He had been hoping to have some time to gather his thoughts before she got home and steel himself against her inevitable advances to distract him.

"I took the night off," she responded casually. She was lounging on the long wraparound couch in the den, shoving handfuls of white cheddar popcorn into her mouth from a huge economy-sized bag that sat on the floor in front of her.

"Why?"

"Just wanted to," was her muffled response. She took a swig from her bottle of Sprite. Kyle noticed she was avoiding his eyes.

Kyle pulled the ottoman directly in front of her and sat down, looking right into her eyes.

"You're blocking the TV, Kyle," Wanda said, trying to wave him away with her hand. She still wouldn't look right at him.

Kyle ignored her. "You wanna tell me why you went and told Sahara about my plan to get custody of Rison?" The edge in his voice was evident.

Wanda chewed slowly, thinking of a good enough answer. She hadn't expected him to find out about that so soon. She had *just* told Sahara about that a few hours earlier. Little Miss Sahara didn't waste any time running to Kyle, did she?

"I just felt she had a right to know," she finally responded, her voice low.

"Since when did you care about Sahara?"

"Uh, since birth. She *is* my cousin, Kyle, or did you forget?"

"Did you? 'Cause you certainly weren't thinking about that when you seduced me when I was still married to her, at our anniversary party, no less. Not to mention intentionally keeping me from seeing my own daughter, who is also your cousin, which you might as well not even bother continuing trying to deny."

"I know Rison is my cousin."

"I'm talking about you trying to keep me from seeing her, Wanda. Don't play."

Wanda sighed. "Why would I do that?"

"I don't know, Wanda. Why *would* you do that?"

"You're being ridiculous, baby. I've told you time and time again that I have no intention of trying to come between you and your daughter."

"Yeah, that's what you *said*. But now I'm wondering how much of what you say is believable."

Wanda looked at him finally. "All because I went and talked to Sahara?"

"No. All because you went and talked to Sahara about something I specifically asked you not to talk to her about. And you might as well keep all this stuff about you just looking out for your cousin and anything like that, 'cause I'm not buying it for a minute."

Wanda figured she might as well come out with it. This didn't seem like a time when she could make him forget about everything with a few coy words and a flash of her thong. His anger was written all over his face and she figured that only the truth would stand any chance in erasing it.

He'll forgive me regardless, she thought to herself, sitting up on the couch. *He always does.*

"All right, Kyle," she said, placing a hand on each of his legs. "Here it is. I'm sorry if you think I betrayed your trust, but I didn't know what else to do. You had become so obsessed with Sahara's personal life that I got a little jealous. I had to do *something* to get your mind back on me and us."

"Did that something include taking Sahara's name out of my phone?"

Wanda glanced at the ground before looking back at him. "Yeah, I did that. I figured if you didn't talk to her, you'd forget about her."

Kyle's face screwed up into a twisted mangle of incredulousness and anger. "Are you *kidding* me?? She's the mother of my child, Wanda. I was married to her for eight years. You couldn't have seriously thought that doing something like erasing her name out of my phone would make me forget about her."

"What can I say, Kyle? I was desperate. And desperate people don't always think clearly or make the best decisions."

"Obviously."

"I just wanted things to go back to the way they were in the beginning," she continued seductively, sliding her hands up his thighs. "When we used to be all about each other. All we cared about what being together. It was like we were already on our honeymoon. You remember, baby?"

Kyle just sat there looking at Wanda, seeing her in a whole new light. At that moment, he wasn't attracted to her at all.

There was a time when he would spring to attention with her easing her hands towards his crotch the way she was. But now he was unaffected by it.

Probably because he was starting to realize what Wanda was: new ass. As crass as it sounded, it was true. She was a new, unchartered, voluptuous, incredibly insatiable and freaky piece of ass, and he had simply gotten caught up in it. She had reappeared in his life at the right time; when he was bored with his wife and too lazy to actually do something about it. Wanda put out the bait and he jumped at it. Even though he already had something perfectly good at home, a woman most men would fight over, he just had to have something new. And the fact that she was Sahara's cousin also made her forbidden, which probably added to the intrigue. But now the intrigue was starting to wear off.

"Speaking of honeymoons," Wanda continued, still inching her hands towards Kyle's crotch, "I went ahead and made a move for our wedding. I booked a venue today."

Kyle's face was starting to hurt, he was frowning so hard. "You did what? What would compel you to do something like that on your own?"

"You were pussyfooting about it so I just did it myself. What's the big deal? We always planned to get married, anyway, and I probably would have been the one making the decisions about all the details like the venue and stuff, right?"

Wanda was on her knees now, her left hand squeezing and massaging Kyle's manhood through his slacks and the right one working its way under his untucked blue button-down shirt. She leaned in and started licking on his neck, ignoring his angry oblivion. She thought she could get him to come around now, since she was being so honest. "It was time to make some moves, baby. That's why I went ahead and quit my job today."

It took a second for Kyle to register what she said, but when he did, he pushed her away from him, furious, and stood up. He couldn't have heard her right. "What did you just say?"

Wanda was surprised by his reaction. She honestly didn't expect him to get so angry, especially with the way she was touching him. He had never been so upset with her before. Really, upset wasn't even the word; he was *pissed*. And for the first time, she actually took his anger seriously.

"Um, I quit my job."

"You mean you put in notice? So you can go right back up there and renounce it. Take the notice back."

Wanda looked away. "I didn't give any notice, Kyle. I just quit."

Kyle just stood there, looking down at her, wondering how things got to this point. How could he have left a beautiful, loyal, trustworthy, genuinely sweet woman for someone like Wanda? He was too old to be letting his penis make decisions for him, but that's exactly what he had done.

He had allowed himself to be seduced into leaving his wife and child, and had convinced himself that it was because he loved Wanda, all because he didn't want to put in the needed work on his marriage. He'd told himself Wanda was better suited for him. But he was kidding himself. Wanda wasn't the right woman for him, and she was proving it now. The scheming, the going behind his back, the total disregard for his wishes, not to mention his intelligence, all proved it. He had to wonder what else she had been dishonest about.

There was no way he could be with a woman like Wanda; he couldn't be with someone he didn't trust.

This is what he had left his family for. And now he was kicking the hell out of himself for it.

"That was a big mistake, Wanda," he droned, his voice devoid of emotion. He stepped away from her.

"Baby, really, what is the big deal? I mean, it was inevitable, right? It shouldn't make any difference if I quit before the wedding or after it. We're gonna be together in the end either way."

"No," Kyle said quickly, shaking his head emphatically. "No, we're not."

Wanda's eyes widened. "What?"

"There isn't going to be any wedding. There isn't even going to be any more relationship. We're done."

Wanda grabbed for his leg but he moved away. She *never* expected him to leave her. This wasn't the way it was supposed to go. She was supposed to *always* get her way. That's how it had been with every man *before* Kyle and that's how she expected it to be *with* Kyle, and with any man she might choose to be with after she and Kyle were married, should she choose to go that route. The plan had all been worked out and was going smoothly; she was supposed to take her perfect cousin Sahara's man, make him fall for her, get him to marry her, and then enjoy the good life, doing whatever she wanted while not having to worry about kids or divorce. Those two things were just not an option.

But now, things were falling apart and Wanda was starting to think there wasn't anything she could do about it.

"Kyle, baby, please! I'm sorry!"

"Save it."

"This won't happen again, I promise!"

"It can happen as many times as you want it to, but it won't be with me." He headed towards the kitchen.

Wanda reached her hand out to him, trying to summon tears to her eyes. "Kyle..."

"It's about trust, Wanda. And I obviously can't trust you. You have thirty days to move out." He left the room, leaving her there on the floor.

Wanda couldn't believe it. He was serious. She looked down at her left hand, the sparkling two-carat princess cut yellow diamond gleaming on her ring finger. *At least I get to keep the ring*, she thought to herself.

Almost as if on cue, Kyle reentered the room and walked right over to her, lifting her left hand and removing the ring from her finger. She just sat there, her mouth hanging open, as Kyle walked back out of the room without a word.

CHAPTER TWENTY-TWO

Sahara was trying to get herself back on track. She had let a lot of things come unraveled during the past couple of months and now it was time to put it all back together.

The first thing she did was pray and ask God's forgiveness for her recent actions; her selfishness, the neglect of her child, the causal sex, and missing church because of it. Looking back on it, she didn't even recognize herself.

Julia and Charlie were also due profound apologies. She had taken advantage of them, misusing their encouragement and willingness to be there for her. They were more than willing to forgive her, and she counted herself thankful to have a mother and a friend like them in her life.

She also went and personally apologized to all of her clients for her unprofessional behavior, and was thankful when they forgave her, as well. She didn't know what she had been thinking, jeopardizing her business and livelihood like she did. And all because she wanted to go out and act like an irresponsible teenager. It might've been fun while it lasted, but it was time to act like the grown woman that she was again.

In keeping with that, the main person Sahara owed apologies to was her daughter. Her precious four-year-old little girl had suffered the most because of her irresponsible behavior. Whenever Sahara thought about Rison saying that she didn't want to live with her, it brought tears to her eyes. Those were truly words that she never ever wanted to hear from her child, especially this young. If she needed any motivation to get her things back in order and her priorities straight, that was it.

Rison became her main priority again, just like she had been before Sahara began all the dating. She would pick Rison up from school, help her with her homework, and they would spend quality time together doing things like going to the park, baking brownies, and playing the latest game Rison had made up. Sahara realized how much she had missed her little girl. She had been living in the same house with her, but it was like she hadn't even been seeing her for being so focused on what she wanted, or what she *thought* she wanted. Rison had become a mere obligatory part of her life, like doing chores or paying bills. And just like she would like to do with those things, she had been more than willing to pawn Rison off on somebody else. Sahara was just thankful that she realized what she was doing before too much damage was done to their relationship. She wanted to do whatever it took to make this up to Rison.

The first step towards this was eliminating some of her distractions, and that included breaking things off with Jacob and Tony. As much as she liked them, it just wasn't worth it. They were taking too much of her time and energy, and she obviously didn't have the discipline to deal with it all. She had jumped head-first into the multiple-men dating game with no experience and had let it take her away. She got caught up. It was something she could admit and something she could rectify.

Neither Jacob nor Tony was thrilled that she broke things off with them, but they could respect it because she had been honest with them from the beginning. Part of Sahara could admit that she would miss Tony's kisses and Jacob's spine-tingling sex, but other things were more important. She wanted *one* man in her life, if any, and she wanted to see where things could go with Shannon. He was the one man who never tried to push any kind of physical relationship with her before he really knew her. He was pleased when she told him that she wanted to see him exclusively.

"That's like music to my ears," he had said, giving her that gorgeous grin of his. "You know I was willing to wait for you, right?"

"Yeah, you proved that," Sahara responded. "That's why I wanted to stay with you. I appreciate your patience."

"Precious things are worth waiting for," he said, stroking the underside of her chin. Sahara blushed.

Shannon took her face in his large hands, looking adoringly into her light brown eyes. "So, I'm your man now?" A small smile graced his lips.

"I guess so," Sahara responded shyly with a smile of her own.

"So that means I can do more of this," he whispered, dropping his head and putting his lips on hers. It wasn't their first kiss but it sure felt like it. Sahara wanted to melt when he wrapped her up in those big, strong arms of his and kissed her like he had been waiting for her all his life. She could feel his respect and appreciation for her in that kiss. And she returned it with all of the same that she had for him. Her body responded to him, but not *just* her body; her soul did, as well. She knew she had made the right decision.

· · · ·

KYLE CALLED SAHARA a day or two later and asked if he could come and see Rison. Sahara readily agreed.

Rison was thrilled to see Kyle. She ran into his arms as soon as Sahara told her he was there. It was like the past couple of months of him not coming to see her had never happened. All that mattered was that he was there now. Kyle hugged his baby girl close to him, his eyes tearing up. He hadn't even realized how much he really missed her until she was in his arms. It tore him up that he had let someone like Wanda come between him and his daughter. That would never, ever happen again, with anybody.

He was also thankful that Rison was still young enough to so easily forgive and forget. Had she been a teenager, he might still be putting in some work to get back into her good graces. But now, all he had to do was show up.

Sahara just stood off to the side, smiling at the scene. She watched as Kyle held Rison's tiny hands in his and apologized for not seeing her more. He promised to do better. Sahara got a little choked up when Rison touched his face and said, "I forgive you, Daddy." She could tell Kyle was getting emotional, too, and that wasn't really like him.

"Mommy," Rison called out, climbing onto the sofa, "Does that mean that we can all live together again now?"

Sahara looked at Kyle as she sat next to Rison on the couch. She wanted to be honest but she hated to disappoint her again. Thankfully, Kyle stepped in.

"Listen, sweetheart," he said, sitting on her other side, "Your mommy and I are still divorced, so I'm still going to be living in another house. But that doesn't mean I won't be coming to see you and spending time with you like I used to."

"But why you two get divorced?" Rison asked, looking at him with wide eyes.

Sahara held her breath. This was one question that Rison had never asked. Kyle stepped up again.

"I hurt your mommy," he admitted, glancing up at Sahara. "And now I have to pay for it. But we both still love you very, very much. That's never going to change."

"That's right," Sahara agreed.

Rison looked back and forth between Kyle and Sahara. "How come you can't just tell Mommy you're sorry?" she asked Kyle.

"That's not a bad idea, actually," Kyle said, turning to look Sahara right in her eyes. Sahara looked back at him in mild surprise. "Sahara, I am sincerely, truly sorry for what I did to you. I just recently realized what a mistake I made. I really hope you can forgive me."

Sahara placed her hand on her chest, touched by her ex-husband's words. She could feel the sincerity in his words and she appreciated them more than she could say. She reached over and hugged Kyle; the first hug they had shared in over a year, even since before she found out about his infidelity. Rison just sat in the middle, looking back and forth between them. When Sahara pulled away, she smiled as tears streamed down her cheeks. She wiped her eyes.

"Thank you for that, Kyle," she said, pulling Rison to her and hugging her. "That's all I ever wanted."

Thanks so much for reading! This is an oldie but goodie that I still puts a smile on my face, and I hope it did the same for you, at some point.

If you liked this story, please consider leaving a review. And if you want to show *extra* love, share that you read it on social media! ☺

You can find me on Instagram and TikTok at @authorjessicaterry and on Twitter at @itsJessicaTerry. And don't forget to subscribe to my email list at jessicaterry.com.

Also by Jessica Terry

Don't miss out!

Visit the website below and you can sign up to receive emails whenever Jessica Terry publishes a new book. There's no charge and no obligation.

https://books2read.com/r/B-A-NVYK-WADGB

BOOKS 2 READ

Connecting independent readers to independent writers.

About the Author

Jessica Terry caught the writing bug at a young age and loves little more than holing up at home in Douglasville, GA, cranking out contemporary novels. And eating.

Another thing she loves is interacting with her readers. Sign up for her email list and keep up to date with new releases at www.jessicaterry.com.

Read more at https://www.jessicaterry.com/.